RETURNING FROM
THE UNDERGROUND

RETURNING FROM THE UNDERGROUND

Fritz Glockner

Translated by Elizabeth Polli

Zompopos
El libro es un Zompopo

RETURNING FROM THE UNDERGROUND

Original title: *Veinte de cobre*

Copyright © Fritz Glockner, 1996

Translation from the Spanish: © Elizabeth Polli, 2016

© This edition: Élitro Editorial del Proyecto Zompopos, 2017
   http://editorialzompopos.blogspot.com/
   E-mail: AlaEditorial@zompopos.org

Cover photo: "*View from a hallway into a cell at the West Virginia State Penitentiary, a retired, gothic-style prison in Moundsville, West Virginia, that operated from 1876 to 1995*" by Carol M. Highsmith.
Photo used with the expressed permission of the photographer.

ISBN 10: 0-9788597-7-4
ISBN 13: 978-0-9788597-7-0

Printed in the United States / Impreso en EE.UU.

To the family that understands adversity and its lotteries: Napoleón, Gloria, Ligia, Nadia, D. Napoleón, Enrique.

For Judith and the granddaughters smiling at life.

And for Guadalupe, for her determination.

He who has seen hope,
doesn't forget it.
He looks for it under the skies
and among men,
and dreams that one day he will find it anew,
somewhere.
The possibility of being beats in each man,
or more precisely,
of once again becoming another man.

Octavio Paz

The only thing
that can save us
from loneliness
is nostalgia.

Benito Taibo

Contents

Foreword

Somewhat of a ruthless note[1]

When he brought me that very first draft I asked myself: "Should I tell him the truth, or should I just pat him on the back?"

Fritz Glockner had told me: "I'm going to write a novel with my father as the main character."

My initial reaction was *distance yourself* and I began to talk about the Romans. How much do you know about the Romans? You know nothing about either the Romans or Julius Cesar. How much do you know about your father? To start writing a novel like that you'd have to sit yourself down and do your research, not only about what you remember, what you don't remember, what you know, what you don't know, what the context was . . .

But who was I to give advice? And where did I come up with the Romans and Julius Cesar? I always have the feeling that when you tackle a topic, you struggle with distance and proximity, the two ways to approach a story. When Fritz told me he was ready to write a novel about his father, I was just about, but just about, to try with all my might to convince him not to. I did in fact try twice. The first time I was so convincing that he was paralyzed for months, because I let him have it, I told him to be careful, be careful because it's a topic that can drive you crazy. Literature needs distance; proximity is not a good companion. You don't want to go down that testimonial path. You could, but you really don't want to.

Then there was the second time the manuscript landed in my hands. Proof of Fritz's tenacity. And that's a virtue that is not extra-literary but literary. I read the first few pages of the novel and told him: "Do you want the truth, or do you want me to keep it to myself?" "I want the truth." That was a suicide mission because I am ruthless. I told him that I thought it was a piece of shit: it was poorly narrated, the chronology was off, the subjects were off, the counterpoint between past and present failed; it was a disaster. You are trapped by testimonial and you can't let the literature flow. But you know what? Don't pay any attention to me. I always end my sentences like that, "but don't pay any attention to me." It's a dishonest way of saying: I don't want to be responsible for going around telling anyone to write or to stop writing. Let your Mother tell you, or the God of all atheists, or something like that. Not me, I don't want that responsibility.

But Fritz is stubborn. The third time the manuscript landed in my hands, I didn't know whether to say yes or no to him. And here I'm criticizing myself—I didn't dare start it. The fourth time he showed me his novel it was in book form already. So, it wasn't my fight anymore; you've published it, it's on paper. Thus, it was with great serenity that I could sit down and read *Returning from the Underground*. It surprised me: it was a very interesting first novel. You could tell, in my humble opinion, that it was a first novel. It lacked a bit of literary purpose, due to the dreadful combination of testimonial and the purest narrative freedom, less caught up with the story that had to be told, when you're obligated to explain what really happened with characters, names, citizens, and situations. There's a type of trap in testimonial that forces the characters to turn to the left and not in the direction a novel needs them to go, to the right. They couldn't have been in a good mood that day because I remember they were in a bad mood. It wasn't Friday, it was Saturday. There is a kind of imprisonment imposed by testament that inhibits literature from unfolding; it's tied down by the smallest details. It's very difficult to find a way to combine testimonial material with the freedoms of creation, the ones that allow you to let a secondary character develop, for example, or let you go down a lateral path and strengthen a plot. I think you can see this—the testimonial constraint can still be found in *Returning from the Underground*. And it's a good thing and a bad thing, because the novel weighs toward the side of testimonial, and I believe that testimony is one of the highest forms of art in contemporary Mexican narrative.

It's not coincidental; it isn't accidental that the chronicle has been the great post '68 phenomenon of the history of Mexico. It's not coincidental that the stories are told in first person with the commitment of I am telling it and thus I accept it, with the commitment that I am out in public and this is what I am going to tell everyone. It's not coincidental that the chronicle has been one of the preferred genres of readers in the cultural resurgence after the '68 era we suffered in this country. In opposition to the official story, in opposition to the anonymous story, in opposition to the detached story, chronicle as first-person narrative. I think it is a fact that has to do with the need to go back and retell [the story of] this country we live in, beginning with the acceptance that there are credible and non-credible witnesses and establishing this relationship of credibility with the reader.

On the one hand, *Returning from the Underground* brings together the virtues of testimony and at the same time it enters into a very conflictive field, the field of family love, father-son relationships, and more importantly relationships of absence. Add to that one of the most aggravating elements, the political multiplier: the history of the guerrilla, the dirty war, the disappearances. It's prickly material and I think it's a very difficult book, yet it's well resolved. Very difficult, well resolved, because you absorb the interference with the purely personal. That is what will move all of you readers when you read it, as it did me when I read it, the weight of personal relationships: the elements of loss, of confusion, of who is he and who am I, the lost character (a great literary theme), an author searching for that great character, in this case his father. That is what makes this book require a second reading, because today in Mexico we don't want just a first reading anymore, we want a literature of a first and a second reading. We don't only want them to tell us about the small passions in life, we want them to tell us the stories about the great passions. And it's an indirect story. It uncovers just a bit about the dirty war of the 1970s, a dirty war that hasn't been described, a dirty war that horrifies, a dirty war that brought a few hundred young people that felt the urgent need to change this country, who opted for the quickest and most desperate way, face-to-face with a system whose capacity for evil we all know, a repressive system with diabolic tendencies capable of destroying everything in its path, of torture, of illegally entering people's homes, of assassinating children, of shooting at cribs, of delivering the coup de grace, of torturing people for weeks and months. And this story has not been told; it's a story to which we have applied self-censorship. They aren't going to tell it until the day we send them to trial for their crimes. And we don't want to tell it because it's not entirely our story. The vast majority of us opted for more social ways of fighting, more massive, less face-to-face, or apparently less face-to-face ways. We disassociated ourselves from them. This history of the Mexican dirty war has been a story colored by the hue of shame, of "I better not get involved, in the end they were all a little crazy, not just some of them." And I don't think it's a topic worth the argument of avoiding, I don't think there is any topic one can avoid. I think that the only way to examine this country is to examine it as a whole and not piece-by-piece and I think that the second reading of Fritz's novel is the one that contributes to the narrative of the dirty war of that period.

I won't go on and on. As I rewrite this note, the author is no longer debuting. Many books have followed *Returning from the Underground*. The function of a book presentation is to encourage people to read the book. No presentation is going to make a book better, especially this one: a story well told, a powerful story, a terrible story, a candid story, a beautiful story, and on top of that it's well written. It's worth coming face-to-face with it, because it's our story as well.

Paco Ignacio Taibo II

[1]Paco Ignacio Taibo II delivered these remarks on April 30, 1996, in Coyoacán, Mexico, D.F., the day *Veinte de cobre* was released. With Taibo's permission, his remarks have been transcribed, and subsequently translated, and serve as the *Foreword* to this translated edition.

Part 1

LIFE IS A NOVEL

It sucks talking to you about the ghosts you discovered. Without really wanting to, you realized that you had a past you knew nothing about. Finding that document on the bookshelf in the bedroom probably wasn't the best way to face the story we hid for such a long time. Those dates, events, people and photographs of a place you didn't recognize—they didn't seem to have anything to do with you.

Those yellowed newspapers weren't the best way to discover the truth either. How could you have known what was waiting for you in the archives? Maybe there, my dear Irving, you found irrelevant stories that made you nervous. Each note carried your collective past and the emotions your family lived through.

You finally found the father you never knew, the father you never had, with the exception of those few odd, fleeting references. The only thing you did remember were the endless hallways filled with people. You were four years old and it was a shock when we placed you in front of an unknown man who was living in that dark building. We all waited anxiously for your answer, your reaction.

"It's Papa," you heard someone say.

Scared, the only thing you could say was that you didn't like Papa's school, you wanted to leave and never return. Since then you haven't gone back to Lecumberri.

Later, when that man was freed from jail, he had so many things to consider. He had to organize his existence, re-familiarize himself with the family he had abandoned, give explanations, and assimilate back into society. He had practically no time for you. Occasionally the man with the moustache arrived with books for his youngest son; books with titles like "The Chinese Circus," or "How Children See the Moncada." These publications you guarded jealously, as they were your only point of reference to understanding your father.

One day we told you that this stranger, your father, had suffered an accident, and that you would never see him again. In any case, you never had time to miss him. Your encounters had been so sporadic that simply seeing him had never become normal. It's possible that you felt sad or nostalgic, a bit infected by the atmosphere that seized your surroundings, but you didn't suffer. In spite of the fact that you had every right to know what had happened, no one in the family had time for you. I know now that it's not easy for you to understand our attempts to forget. Your presence was necessary for us to be able to cope with those adverse times—your games and your innocence kept our family united. It'll take time for you to understand the shock, why we marginalized you in the past, and above all, to understand the way you met him. I guess it sucks opening a newspaper after fifteen years and discovering the mutilated face of the person they called your father . . .

On the other hand, there was no opportunity to understand his motives, no time to ask him anything. The notes you read included familiar names. You tell me that your indignation and your doubts kept mounting. And you must really feel like getting even . . .

You learned the details about his detention, about his activity in the guerrilla, about the government's lies, why he was gone, the reason you two were strangers. You entered this turbid story through the press, alone and defenseless. The time: two years and eight months. During that time this stranger dedicated little to you. At least we didn't lie about the accident because, of course, there is a huge difference between a car accident and being gunned down in broad daylight. You probably didn't give much weight to that note in red ink. They're always so commonplace and impersonal.

As the youngest of the family you had to live with a false story, one that you are only now discovering. Life may seem, perhaps, like a fabrication, like a novel that someone is trying to force you to believe.

THEY ARRIVED ON TIME, at the agreed-upon hour. That was the day you chose to change your life, in spite of the doubts and the remorse that every once in a while ate away at you for abandoning your family.

"It's for them," you repeated over and over amidst the uncertainty.

All the details seemed to be in place. It was probably not the best time to get involved in the subversive activities that the organization was carrying out, the ones you had supported financially for some time. You were tired, however, of figuring out how to survive even the most absurd hardships. You recalled the last time you lent your support and how harshly they treated you: "The commitment to the destitute, to the people of Mexico, is not Christian charity, it's a duty of conscience, of ideology. You are a passive guerrilla fighter, but just the same you are committed to our cause."

Then came the decision to become active, one you thought about for a long time. In spite of your doubts, no one ordered you to make that decision. You successfully met the requirements of the training exams, you had enough courage to face death, you transformed the personality of many compañeros, you took care of several gun shot wounds and you never missed a weekly training. It seemed ridiculous that at your age you were following the local fairs simply to get some practice at target shooting, but it was the best way to prepare without spending a lot of money.

"It's time," you heard them say from behind the door.

Your case was exceptional. Few people with a relatively

comfortable status, at your age and with a family made this kind of decision. Few dare to put ideals above all, to leave all behind: friendships, family, business. You had asked yourself many times where these utopian ideals could lead.

"Are you ready?" the young man who walked into your office asked you, knowing full well that in order to make the connection time was of the essence.

"Let's go," you managed to say before looking around for the last time at the walls, the desk, the shelves, the decor in the room. You knew there was no option to turn back, the decision you had made was forever. The prize for the game you were about to begin was life or death, even though the starting place seemed common enough. Today you would change your name and your past. Nothing you were leaving behind mattered, you were about to become another person: Miguel Ángel would disappear as soon as you got into the car that was waiting outside. A person dedicated to changing the unjust structures of this country, one dedicated to the armed movement, was about to be born.

You gave your secretary an envelope. She knew beforehand that she was to give it to your wife—it contained the alleged reason that would justify your absence from that point on. You said goodbye at roughly eleven o'clock in the morning. The young man who was waiting for you wanted to understand you. You didn't know him, that's how it had to be. For everyone's safety, contact with the organization was made through specific channels, no one knew the members of the other cells. You put your briefcase, which held a change of clothes, under your arm. It was your only luggage. No one should know that you were going on a trip.

You got into the car, followed by the young man who spoke to you as if you had known each other forever. Your actions were mechanical. All your muscles were stiff and a false smile was pasted on your face. Acting normal was the best guarantee as the police might show up to interview the employees of the hospital. Your family, worried, would look for some way to escape this nightmare because the reasons you gave in the letter might not have justified your leaving. All the options had been considered. You had to follow the script step by step and leave nothing to chance.

Before long, the car that was carrying you away to a new life took the old road to Mexico City. The countryside made you feel safe. The trees that lined the way bade you a sweet farewell. The pretending was over. The person accompanying you let you sink deeply into your thoughts. He turned on the radio to make the trip easier for you.

Just ten days had passed since the massacre in Mexico City, on Avenida de los Maestros. That Holy Thursday was still present in the national newspapers. The young man at the wheel showed his indignation, his pain—one of his brothers had lost his life at the hands of the paramilitary group, *los halcones*. You didn't know what to say. The driver interpreted your silence.

When you reached Río Frío he stopped the car. You didn't know where he was taking you. You went into a truck stop.

"We're going to eat something, and when I'm finished I'll get up and leave. Fifteen minutes after I've gone, you'll leave and take the next bus to Mexico City and get off at the outskirts. At the first traffic light on Avenida de Zaragoza a grey Chevrolet will be waiting for you. You'll give this envelope to the person in the car, and he will continue guiding you."

You listened attentively to the instructions, nervous because of your lack of experience. You thought someone might have overheard, but the truck drivers were busy eating their lunch, the music was too loud for eavesdropping and the young man acted with ease. You didn't speak to each other again until he left.

"Good luck," was the last thing you heard him say before he left you alone.

You waited while you finished your cup of coffee, calm to those around you, until the fifteen minutes had passed. When the time was up you paid the bill and waited five more minutes until the bus to Mexico City arrived.

You settled in among the chickens, baskets, sacks, hats and toys, ready to continue the trip. You had never traveled to Mexico City like this before. The common people were there with you, the oppressed for whom you were changing your way of life.

A little more than an hour and a half later the bus reached the outskirts. When you got off the Avenida de Zaragoza seemed different, you discovered buildings you had never seen before. The designated car was at the first traffic light. Even though everything lined up, your lack of experience made you hesitate. You traveled the distance that separated you from the car, you double-checked that the indicated person was inside, and you felt for the envelope hidden in your jacket as you reached the window on the driver's side. A lazy hand gestured out the window and took the password.

"Shall we go?" was the answer you got in exchange for the envelope. Still suspicious, you got in.

"I'm the right person, don't worry. Was the trip difficult?" he asked, to alleviate the tension that dominated you.

"A little trying, nothing too bad."

You decided to hide the feelings that traveling in a second-class bus had brought up. The excitement made you forget your previous thoughts and you began to take on the personality of the character you would be from that day on. You tried to stop worrying about your past, about the people you were abandoning. You had to do things right you told yourself—arrive on time, see the appropriate people, and have the password ready. Those were the things you were obsessed with at that moment.

The second guide turned out to be more of a talker. He distracted you so much that you didn't notice how far you had traveled until you stopped for a moment at the second tollbooth on the Mexico City to Querétaro highway.

"You'll be at the first safe house for just two months," he started to give you your initial instructions. He gave you a new name, he handed you an identification card, he listed the norms you should learn by heart, the phone number to call in case of an emergency. He gave you a gun, he took all the money you had on you, and he explained the different ways to dye your hair.

"Don't write anything down," he repeated over and over again. "You're going to get out at the restaurant just past Querétaro. Next to the gas station there's a parking lot, there'll be a wood-paneled van there, you're going to tell the driver where you're coming from, your new name, and he'll take you to where you should go. Welcome to the fight."

Once again you felt nervous. This way of welcoming you in brought you back to reality. You hurriedly put what the second young man had given you into your briefcase. The car stopped and you went straight to the bathroom at the restaurant. Maybe urinating would alleviate the tension. You didn't see the motor mouth depart. When you left the restaurant you walked toward the van parked next to the gasoline station, and the new driver knew it was you as you approached. You had seen him before, when he had picked up some of your contributions. You followed instructions, talking for a moment outside the van. He then asked you to get in the back door, put on the blindfold that another *compañero* in the van would give you, get comfortable and for the moment not to talk to the other two people that were, just like you, in the van.

His attitude seemed a bit strange. You didn't trust him at first but later you understood those extreme security measures.

You took your place in the van. You didn't have time to see the two *compañeros* who, along with you, were passing over to the underground. The trip was long, your thoughts ran wild the whole way, the struggle with the past that you had to erase started up once again.

Different images came to mind—feelings of anxiety, insecurity, fear, and remorse invaded you. For a moment you were ashamed of these feelings. Even though you were conscious that this had been your choice, and even thought you had company, the silence and that hint of loneliness you felt added to the unknown of what awaited you. It made you realize that beyond any ideology, beyond the balls you had (or didn't have) you were just one more fucking human being with normal imperfections and weaknesses. Super heroes don't exist, not even in the cartoons your kids watched. It helped you a bit to believe that your two travel companions would be feeling the same. Misery likes company. You repeated the saying over and over, the saying that your father and partner, the ex-president of the university—the legend—always repeated. You felt you had the obligation to forget him as well.

Night had fallen by the time the van finally stopped. "We're here," shouted the driver, as the second *compañero* opened the door, the one who had sat next to the new underground members. He helped you stretch out your muscles, stiff from anxiety, the uncomfortable trip, the adrenaline. You took your blindfold off and you were surprised that one of your *compañeros*, recently recruited, was a young girl. She could have been the age of one of your daughters. The safe house was in the middle of a large tract of land.

"Come in and eat, you must be starving," another young man said as he welcomed you in a tone so familiar that it surprised you. It unleashed all the tension accumulated during the trip.

The conversation at dinner was a bit forced, and since you couldn't talk about the past, there were few common topics other than the cause.

It was past 9:00 p.m. when they showed you to your rooms

and gave you the necessary information to survive the training period.

When you lay down you were sure it would be hard to fall asleep. The decision had been difficult. You felt the empty space next to you in bed and rubbed shoulders with it. The only thing you wanted was to share that feeling with the night.

Militia est vita. The slogan of the Jesuit school where you had studied many years ago came to mind. Without even realizing it you let yourself be carried away by the exhaustion of the trip and of so much pent up nervousness, and contrary to your predictions, you fell asleep almost immediately. Your training would start the next day.

I RAN DESPERATELY, aimlessly at times, just so I could hold onto something. Papa could be on any corner—all faces became his.

Imagination and necessity allow you to change reality at your convenience. You've been thrown onto a stage and you don't even know the role you're supposed to play. Every once in a while you discover eyes in the walls, shadows in the windows. I wanted to collide with him because his voice was becoming more and more distant.

All of a sudden the only thing you have left is reality, presence living in memory. The shadow lies in wait yet doesn't grow, it simply follows you. It doesn't let you be, it simply chases you.

When I turned ten I wanted a lot of birthday presents, but most of all I wanted one from Papa. Maybe that day was when I understood what the word 'abandonment' meant.

Mama was at the beauty parlor; I had gone to the store next door. Collecting stamps was in fashion. That was when we played, "yes, yes, yes I have that one, noooooooooooooo!"

María showed up in the street all of a sudden, her face holding back the happiness. It seemed like she wanted to shout. I deciphered her emotions as best I could, and imagined what was happening. Without even talking to her I began to run as fast as I could. Three blocks separated our house from the beauty parlor and the store. I ran frenetically. I didn't care if cars were driving down the street or not, I had little time.

When I arrived I didn't stop ringing the bell. No one answered, so I went in through the bathroom window. When I was half way in, the door to the street opened: Papa was there.

We hugged. I so wanted to scold him for not getting me a present on my birthday. Maybe he had an explanation. Time was of the essence—we couldn't waste it on meaningless anger. The tears welled up in our eyes.

Someone knocked at the door. Mama and María were in the street. It took me a while, but I opened it.

In the stairway, where I had hugged my father, only my memories remained.

There's nothing like the television when you want to lull yourself to bed and sleep soundly.

What we never imagined was that it was that habit that allowed us to learn of Papa's whereabouts.

David and I were fast asleep while Zabludovksy was talking on the screen. Mama and our sisters were having dinner in the dining room, and I think it was Mama who asked Adriana to go to our room and turn the television off.

Coincidences are times and places that can't be repeated, and occasionally some prefer to hang the title of miracles on them.

When Adriana got to our room to turn off the TV, the news broadcaster was announcing the arrest of twenty guerrilla fighters. Curiosity got hold of Adriana and before turning it off she listened to the report. When she heard Papa's name she called Mama immediately. Mama was a bit reticent to heed her daughter's call.

It's curious how one forgets that behind any news story there are human beings who suffer and cry. You get used to learning about things by remembering your surroundings. You ignore the men and their feelings until in some way you belong to what happened.

When he was finished, Zabludovsky repeated Papa's name. Adriana had heard right, there was no room for doubt. After two years and eight months we had some news—he had disappeared, he had abandoned us—and now, just like that, he was on TV!

And on top of it he was under arrest and charged with conspiracy, forgery of documents, carrying military-grade firearms and associating with criminals. If it hadn't been for those few minutes no one would have known anything about his whereabouts.

It sucks that reality erupts into your life through a TV screen that you usually relate to in such an impersonal way. Sitting in front of the box you are a witness to events that seem fictitious, where everything will always be detached from you and your family. As much as Mama and my sisters have described that night I can't imagine what they felt, how they reacted, the way they pretended to fall asleep after knowing the state Papa was in.

Don't think that you were the only one who was taken by surprise. After the news, so many feelings were suppressed by each of the women in our family. I suppose it was one of the longest nights of your life. To have the information and at the same time no power to do anything about it. Helplessness is the worst company, especially at night.

I remember that Mama woke me up very early the next day. When I opened my eyes, her calm face awaited me with the news.

"It's better for me to tell you than for you to find out from someone else." She didn't want to frighten me, she wanted to bring me up to date with what was happening as delicately as possible, and her soft words didn't alarm me. Mama knew what Papa meant to me, so she used extreme caution while filling me in on the details.

"Your father is in prison."

All of a sudden the meaning of the news wasn't important. Not the place, not the prison and its environment of assassinations, violence, terrorism . . . The mere fact that we knew something about him provoked a violent emotion. The anxiety caused by his absence and the lack of a paternal figure I had searched for so many times pounded in my head. At that moment not even the accusations, several times rehearsed, came to mind.

The need to have news about Papa was always present in our lives. At that moment knowing where he was and having the opportunity to see him again was like forcing an adolescent to understand what it was like living without a father. Later a strange sensation invaded me: in spite of everything, don't believe what they are telling you.

I asked Mama for further explanations. During those hours she didn't have any other details, she just told me to go and get as many different newspapers as I could. I got up immediately and left the house, I went to the closest newsstand and came back with the newspapers that you recently discovered. It was just a pile of printed-paper in which we found out about Papa and his situation, about that man who some time ago had played with me, defended me, put up with my tantrums.

I've thought, many times, about which of the three brothers has been luckier—David and you for never having lived with our father, or me, who had him and lost him more than once.

María and Aunt Emma had gone to Mexico City early in order to see Papa. David went to grandfather's house to inform him of what we knew at that point, and only Adriana and Mama waited anxiously for me to get back with the newspapers. You didn't understand what was happening all around you, you only saw us run from one place to the next and when Aunt Rosi arrived she immediately took you away, with some excuse or another, from the bad news. You were only four years old.

As we went through the newspapers, the fear of learning more upset us tremendously. We leafed through each paper quickly and for the first time in my life an article became important. At last we came to the page that described all the details of Papa's case. We learned a bit about his reasons for leaving. In the long run, he had exchanged us for his ideals. His decision to participate in an armed movement was the motive.

When we discovered the photograph of his disfigured face we completely forgot about any resentments. It was hard to pick him out. Of the twenty faces that the article printed, the image we held dear of Papa was unrecognizable. It wasn't until then that we understood how fucked he was, how difficult the situation was. A whole variety of feelings overtook us—surprise, happiness, rage, bitterness, anxiety . . .

Adriana and I couldn't hold back the anger anymore and we exploded into tears. We hugged and tried to console each other. Mama, surprised by the events, was trying to understand what was happening. That photo had to have been a trick, that wasn't Papa, it was impossible that he was the same man we held in our memories. There was no comparison to the wooden bust that was on the bureau in Mama's bedroom, the one that fell on you once and made you mutter: "fucking Dad."

When we saw his disfigured image we tried to discover what was wrong—there had to be something wrong.

The hours went by slowly. A few people were brave enough to visit us after they found out. We anxiously awaited the return of María and Aunt Emma.

Had they found him? Were they able to see him? What was happening? These were the questions that ran through our minds and our bodies during that long wait.

At last, around 7:00 p.m., they arrived from Mexico City. They were both exhausted, and the way they looked was the best indication of the situation Papa was in. They told us everything they had had to go through in order to visit him, and then in order to face him. The atmosphere at the prison, the newspapers stuck to bodies to keep the cold out, his face all swollen from the beatings, the pain reflected in his eyes, the wounds all over him. It had been almost a month since Papa had been arrested and it wasn't until now that he had been brought before the proper authorities and the media.

Without much detail he had told them the ordeal he had been through during the last several days, suffering unimaginable forms of torture. He was paying the price for daring to participate in an armed group, for daring to confront the government. The collective nightmare had just begun. After all, "that game of playing life, it's something that sometimes hurts."

The next day I woke up feeling sick, waiting for any bit of news, experiencing anxiety as a new way of life. Only 24 hours had passed.

YOU KNEW IT WAS FORBIDDEN to write anything down, to leave a written testimony of your acts, but the comfort that activity brought was irreplaceable. You hid it very well, until one day someone found it.

OCTOBER: It's been four months since I've been here. It's been difficult to grow accustomed to it, to situate myself in this new reality. Several times I've doubted whether I did the right thing in participating this way. I know it's irresponsible of me to write these notes, but I'm feeling like a ghost. It's been about 120 days it seems, since I walked away from my past. From time to time, the fact that I abandoned those around me makes me feel uneasy. I'm convinced that I chose the best option, but it is so difficult to assimilate the changes . . . above all at my age.

NOVEMBER: As hard as I tried not to write again it was impossible, mostly because I felt a great relief the last time I did. If someone were to discover these notes I'd receive a sanction. Life has been intense lately, the work very difficult, mostly because I can't get used to it. They say that what is happening to me is normal: I think people recognize me everywhere I go. Every once in a while the idea that I'll run into someone I know and have to give explanations overcomes me.

FEBRUARY: The enemy is all around—we could come upon a snitch on any corner. Our base is very limited. We have to promote more participation in some of the labor unions, student groups and in the *campesino* groups. The political parties have enforced the different strategies they use in order to take control. We cannot trust them.

One of the most important leaders of the *campesino* groups has died. Genaro fell into the trap; the revolutionary forces have been weakening. We must join forces and leave our differences behind. In light of our objectives it seems absurd that we can't.

APRIL: The urban activist has more difficulties than the one who decides to head for the hills. Our identity, as well as the security of the organization, is in trouble. The way we have been raising money seems very slow to me, it's hardly sufficient. The kidnappings and robberies that others have engaged in cannot succeed. The important thing, however, is how society understands these actions. The conscience of the people is too weak to overcome the propaganda campaigns of the government, who label us as common terrorists . . .

AUGUST: I sometimes have arguments with different *compañeros*. I suppose that a lot of this has to do with the age difference. The majority of them are young and they see things differently. Perhaps I am more cautious, less determined.

In any event one has to be disciplined.

SEPTEMBER: The ethical make-up of revolutionary individuals is something that must be focused on over and over again. Time is one more enemy. When will we be able to take control of collective reason?

ALL THE NOTES and all the photos, the anecdotes of the adolescents who lived the decade of the seventies, are on the same bookshelf where you found the articles about Papa.

You ask why we are a ghost generation. Since everything was foreign to us, we simply inherited all that had been handed to us. As Althusser would say: "History had taken over our adolescence."

What can one say about his or her adolescence?

During the seventies, those of us who were at the age of searching, of fighting, of heroic exploits, of girls, Toby's Club had just disbanded, of alcohol, of cigarettes—*Delicados* of course, because *Marlboros* were for the preppies who always screwed their mothers over—we lived more or less with the failures and doubts that other generations had left us.

During those days, when life was a mere pretext to masturbate and to feel tough, we took everything from other generations: music, literature, vices, instructions, fashion, the whole nine yards.

We were neither one thing nor another. We invented bits and pieces from what other generations lent us and we clung to secret hiding places because we knew we were fucked. We belonged to a present that had no answers.

We didn't have any ideals that would send us to the streets to demonstrate and we even grew to be somewhat afraid of freedom. We became domesticated.

And occasionally we were spontaneous. We are ghosts walking around out there, and once in a while we take control of our past, constructing lies in order to know that we exist, in order to be able to realize that life is not always a dream.

Part 2

YOUR LONGING GATHERS IN THE SHADOWS

The meeting was scheduled for 10:00 in the morning. Vicente and Ángeles had already arrived, and they didn't notice anything strange when they knocked on the door. At 10:15 you decided to start without Fabiola and Armando, the only two who were not there. Dora had the coffee ready. Just when you were about to start you heard footsteps, people running everywhere. Someone was walking on the roof of the safe house—you could hear several men climbing the walls. At that moment you didn't know what was happening. No one attempted to take out his or her gun, no one, not even as a security measure.

A bit out of curiosity you went over to a window, confused. It was then that you noticed there were men in civilian dress everywhere, carrying long-range rifles. The shock paralyzed you and the only thing you did was close the curtains, as if that would make what you had seen disappear. You went over to your *compañeros*, sucking in all the air your lungs could hold.

"We're surrounded."

It seemed like no one heard your words. In spite of being prepared to face, at any moment, any type of situation, no one snapped out of the shock. Everything seemed normal—no one tried to defend him or herself, to destroy the archives, to take an offensive stance.

The invaders took over the patio and shouted for you to give up. At that moment everyone wanted to react . . . it was too late, the police had all the exits covered. It was well planned—few of the police wore uniforms. Questions started filling your heads: "What the fuck was happening? How had they found you? What was the mistake? Who was the snitch?" No one was afraid, no one was surprised, as they all knew that sooner or later this could happen. What they never imagined was their own reaction.

They heard the police breaking the windows. The first policemen came in through the bedrooms. In the dining room, you and your *compañeros* hardly had time to exchange glances in silence.

"Everyone's under arrest!" the first officer who arrived in the room, flailing a sawn-off shotgun, shouted. Behind him were a dozen agents. You didn't have time to do anything. You immediately felt the blows all over your bodies.

For a second you thought there was no reason for them to hit you, resisting arrest existed in theory only. The surprise attack had played a bad joke on you. Gender didn't matter to the a-gents—they hit you, Dora and Ángeles with the same rage. The kicks, the blows, the gun butts and the slaps came from everywhere. After the shake-up they tied you up and put your four bodies, which were beginning to feel the pain of the attack, on the living room floor. The agents began to search every corner of the house, destroying everything. Right before your eyes they trashed the few belongings that had been useful to you during your stay in that safe house. They looked for papers, maps, dates, plans, names, addresses, contact information, guns, explosives, anything that proved your existence, the attacks, your stance against the government.

The jackknives destroyed pillows and cushions. Glass objects fell smashing to the ground. A carpet of shattered glass covered the entire floor of the house, together with newspapers, magazines, books and papers that were strewn about everywhere. The noise was phenomenal, just like when drumbeats burst in the middle of a symphony orchestra.

Dora began to cry silently, yet you found no words to console her. You felt guilty; you hadn't reacted in time. Everyone felt the same. You had seen the men dressed as civilians through the window, encircling the house, so why didn't you say so and initiate the resistance?

Fading sirens could be heard in the distance and a loud din filled your ears. Everyone was giving orders. Things kept falling to the floor and your body was beginning to feel the blows you had received. You saw blood flowing from Vicente's nose. Just then your mouth tasted acidic, thick, your lips were split, these sensations had prohibited you from realizing the state you were in. Ángeles' eyes seemed to jump out of their sockets—they reflected hatred toward the police who were destroying everything and mocking you and your ideals.

No one dared utter a word. Immobilized, you observed how the police found the information they wanted. At that moment you didn't really care what happened to you, what awaited you. You and your *compañeros* only wanted to get word, in some way, to the rest of the organization that you had been found out, that you hadn't been able to destroy even the most basic information, that the Monterrey network was in danger. The faintest hope was that Fabiola and Armando had been able to escape and get word out as to what was happening to you.

You lost all sense of time as the pain started to grow in every crack and crevice of your body. The police were ignoring you after the beating, since what they really wanted was to find the information. They wanted the sting to be so big that the organization would fall apart and disappear once and for all.

At last a fat man who appeared to be the boss ordered someone to pick you up and take you to a van, and with much pushing and shoving the order was carried out. You now felt every little thing that touched your body, but none of you dared emit even a moan. When you went outside you found yourselves in the middle of a street filled with curious, wide-eyed onlookers who were trying to figure out what was happening. You went through a mental checklist and everyone in the neighborhood was there: the baker, the butcher, Lolita the tortilla maker, the woman from across the street who was always trying to befriend you and Dora. Several were surprised when they learned that they had been living, for a few months, right next door to terrorists .

"God save us, who would have known?"

"They seemed like such good people."

"If one could only tell by seeing their faces . . ."

You heard all this just before they closed the door to the van and ordered you to lie down on the floor and keep quiet.

You traveled for a long time. Three agents were up front, laughing their heads off, making fun of you. Four more were in the back, stepping on you here and there, celebrating their mission, boasting when they managed to get you to complain. You weren't even able to feel indignant. Meanwhile you saw such hatred on Ángeles' face that it scared you that she might say something, tell them to tell their mothers to go to hell.

The van stopped and they took you into a house. Glancing around quickly, you tried to recognize the neighborhood before they pushed you inside. You had never seen it before, nothing was familiar, but then you realized that hell was far, far away, that your theoretical preparation had been very strong, but it was nothing compared to what you were in for.

They separated you—each of you was put in a different room. You didn't have time to memorize the structure of the house or what the hallway was like, which room you were in, if there were any exits. Once you were in the room with the lime green walls, you realized that your only company would be your own solitude.

You wanted to know which of your *compañeros* was in the room next door, with whom you shared a wall. When the door to your room closed the only things you heard were sporadic footsteps, distant voices, until a series of screams that went on and on made you shudder. You first identified the voice of Ángeles, and for a long time her pain kept you company.

Next it was Dora's voice. It broke your heart to hear her cries for mercy. Your own pain no longer mattered, now your only preoccupation was to pull yourself together so you would have the strength to withstand the torture. It occurred to you that you didn't know any of your *compañeros* very well. Their names were aliases. You compared Ángeles several times to your daughter Adriana—she might even have been the same age. Even though you had become intimate with Dora, you had never asked each other about the past. Your conjugal relationship was strictly for the revolution, period. You didn't have to comprehend anything except the present, the organization, taking control, studying, the ideology. These were people whose stories began once you met them—the past didn't exist. Just like you, they were ignorant about you, your family, your children, where you were from, what you had left behind in order to pass over to the underground.

In between Dora's sobs you remembered all the times you had had to suppress the desire to know more about those around you. It's normal to know things. You justified these thoughts each time. Now you knew that the screams and the pain came from people looking for ideals just like you. Reality always hurts in different ways, though.

Your turn came amidst all the chaos. They didn't take you anywhere, it was right there in your room, that the first of hundreds of interrogations you would suffer took place. Three individuals entered, bringing with them all the necessary tools. At first you weren't afraid. You were a bit disconcerted, your soul and conscience in shambles after having heard Ángeles' and Dora's screams. Your mind went blank, you didn't notice what time it was when they stripped you, or when they hooked the wires up to your testicles, or where they had gotten the water. Every minute, an electrical charge ran through you that sent pain into each and every one of your nerves. Instead of screaming you clenched your teeth. You couldn't think about anything—the pain was so intense that you couldn't even feel it. Your jaw was about to break from the pressure of clenching. The operation was repeated once, twice, three times, and then you lost count. They didn't ask you anything, they just smiled maliciously when your body convulsed from the electrical current. At one point you thought your brain would explode into bits. Your eyes were dilated and you had no time to scream, to cry. You thought you were dreaming—your body vanished. There was no muscle that you didn't feel melting away. You lost consciousness.

"This guy hardly tolerated anything." The sentence reverberated in your room. You managed to hear it when you came to, in spite of the fact that the torturers had left some time ago.

Your mouth was dry—it was impossible to move. You felt like a lifeless doll left alone in some corner. Your torturer had decided to leave you there, on the floor. You had no idea what was happening, you barely recognized the room. For a moment you even forgot your name, your age, your sex, where you were from. You remembered nothing about your life. Time didn't exist in that room with the puppet inside it. The burning in your testicles made you want to look at them. You almost lost it trying to move your head so you gave up. There was not a place on your body that didn't hurt. You tried to close your eyes and you saw a black circle, a hole through which you were falling like a feather.

You became faint, your mouth filled with salty saliva, your stomach began to convulse. When you tried to open your eyes it was too late—a greenish liquid projected out of your bloody mouth. The bitter taste caused more convulsions, making your entire body ache. Then there were the shivers. You were shaking, a marionette shivering. No, it can't be, marionettes don't pee. You felt a stabbing pain take over your penis. Something was dripping out of it, with each drop your soul came out. It burned, it hurt, you pinched yourself, you looked down—there was blood. Puppets don't frighten you thought, and your gaze was lost in the lime green walls. You managed to escape from that horrendous spectacle, from the man you thought was a puppet but was really you. Something had to break away. Your mind wasn't the best thing to lose, and subconsciously you decided that your gaze, fixed on a single point on the lime green wall, could leave and escape as far away as possible.

One, two, seventy-three, one hundred and fifteen hours like that, with your gaze fixed outside of that room. As hard as you fought, your gaze returned to the immensity of the lime green wall in front of you when new screams filled your ears.

You couldn't tell if it was Dora's voice or Ángeles', or even Vicente's. At that moment you were incapable of placing the screams—it was enough simply dealing with your own limp body.

The light in the room went out. Your eyes that had managed to escape for a short time now exploded against a million phosphorescent pin points that hurt deep down and lit up every one of your internal organs. You tried to turn your head, dodging the penetrating points that were like small pins in your pupils. They engulfed you. Your mind didn't explode but it was now flooded with light. You heard in the distance how the torturers' voices turned in your direction.

"Where, you bastard . . . tell us where."

"When, dickhead, when is it going to be...?"

"Who, mother fucker, who is involved in all of this?"

"What were they planning?"

"What else were they going to do, the assholes?"

You made the effort to block the light from your mind.

"The others already gave in, you're the only one left, you bastard."

"Tell us what you know."

Your body had stopped hurting. The light distracted your feelings and your sentiments; it absorbed your nerves. It was impossible to say anything at that moment, absurd to rat on anyone. You didn't utter a word—you didn't give one name, one address. It wasn't so much that you were brave. It was the light that flooded you, that stopped you from remembering anything. It had saturated you to the point that the only thing your mind could do was vomit light.

When you didn't say anything the beatings started all over again. They hit you everywhere; kicks and punches pounded into your body as if you were a punching bag. You didn't even try to cover yourself. The light continued to completely invade you. The first thing you needed to do was get it out of you, to vomit it up, to shit it out. You didn't know when they stopped beating you or when they left you alone. Your pupils took up your entire face—the lime green wall was closer than ever. You knew you were surrounded.

Time passed. Unable to move, you managed to block out the light, only for the pain to come back. Your mind returned and you managed to get control of it. You were your own puppet master. Underneath all that pain you remembered your life and you thought that death was less torturous than what was happening to you.

Images popped into the room. You remembered your family as never before, it had been two years and several months since you'd seen them. You were curious to know how they were, what they thought about you leaving with no explanation. You had children—you were a father—which made you think about your own father. It had been so many years since you had spoken to him. He had told you so many anecdotes: when he was a wrestler cloaked in mask and cape, when he had had to steal food from the market so he could finish medical school and not starve, when he crawled inside that *pulque* barrel during the celebration for some politician. You always doubted whether those stories were true, in spite of the fact that every once in a while his friends backed them up. You knew your father was a legend. It was disconcerting now to think of your half-sister Julia, who was also in the organization. You'd only seen her once since you went underground. The rules were very strict; you hoped she was well, that your arrest wouldn't jeopardize her group, even though you knew nothing at all about where she lived or the work she was carrying out. You couldn't help but worry that the same thing had happened to her. You wanted to cry but you couldn't, it was better when your mind didn't belong to you, when the strings attached to that marionette were pulled by someone else.

"Lunch."

The voice distracted you from your thoughts. You found yourself on the floor and felt your face all swollen. Someone had placed a bowl of what looked like noodle soup in front of you.

"You have to eat something." The voice insisted, but you couldn't place it. "There's still a lot more shit to come and you won't make it on an empty stomach. You've been here for three days," the voice insisted, so you would look up. And you thought it was the same day as the arrest.

You tried to eat a bit of soup, your jaws didn't work, a third of what you spooned into your mouth spilled unwillingly. The metal hurt your cracked lips. It took you a long time to finish that bowl of soup, never mind all that had spilled on the floor and mixed with your urine, bile and blood. The light continued in spite of you having willed it to disappear. It still illuminated you with its brilliance.

Three bowls of soup later the interrogators returned. Now it was time for the mineral water treatment. They sat you down on a wooden chair and tied your hands behind your back. You felt them pull your hair and suddenly, in front of your face, a large man was insistently shaking a bottle of mineral water. He let the gas out slowly and it shot up your nose. You were drowning and for a few seconds you felt your life slipping away. You didn't lose consciousness like before; it was different now. Every time you felt that burst of gas enter your nose you thought your heart was going to blow up—your blood flowed quickly, your lungs filled up with bubbles of gas to the point of exploding.

"Now you understand, asshole!"

You heard the voices, insistent, coming closer to you. Then you discovered that torture was not a way to get you to talk or give up names and addresses. It was merely their game, their manner of having fun, a way to pass the time. It gave them pleasure to see how you twisted and moaned, how your eyes popped out of their sockets.

YOU SPENT TWO WEEKS in that room, coexisting with the different types of torture you had once only heard about but always knew could happen. It was nothing like when you first arrived. Now you too could have fun and enjoy the pain. Now you knew that not all the interrogators lost patience when you didn't respond. You were becoming accustomed to living like this until without advanced warning, they took you away. You were able to discover out of the corner of your eye that the bodies of your *compañeros* were also being transported. They put you in different cars. You weren't afraid at all of what could happen next. You arrived at the police station and you were the first to see the agent. He immediately began the paperwork.

"Name, address, age, marital status . . . "

At first you didn't know what to say, which name to give, which address. For a few seconds you were totally confused, you weren't prepared for this type of questioning. You couldn't identify where your clandestine identity started, when you had stopped being Miguel Ángel and started being Jaime, which of your personalities you should reveal, what that agent knew. Puebla, Monterrey, children, single . . .

"Miguel Ángel . . . " you heard your Puebla name, married with five children. They knew everything, like an all-powerful God. You didn't need to complicate things. They went through the trouble of interrogating you—it was normal procedure. But they knew more about you than you did yourself. They took your fingerprints and your photo. You were assigned to a small cell, from which you saw other prisoners. You thought about the conditions of the others. You were able to exchange a few words with them; they wanted to acknowledge who you were in front of the group, to learn who you really were. You thought you had forgotten the reason you were in that cell.

You spent four days in the county jail in Monterrey. During that lapse of time men who looked like lawyers, who always wore a suit and tie, conducted the interrogations. They kindly took your information, only to have you sign blank papers. You never knew if the words written on those papers were yours or not.

"Out," was the order that soon gave you back your state of anxiety. At least you had had a few minutes of peace. They took you to a armored truck, with bars and metal seats. Later you were transferred along with Dora, Ángeles and Vicente, followed by five soldiers who took their seats and told you immediately not to talk. At first you didn't recognize your compañeros, they had all spent the same amount of time suffering the same ordeal and now they seemed like strangers, distant, deformed. You thought that you must look the same to them, or worse. During the trip you all tried to comfort one another while you could see one another, but no one was really able to pity anyone else.

Not even the shelter of solitude lessened the burden.

You never imagined you would travel from Monterrey to Mexico City handcuffed inside an army truck. That day was dreadful, with your wrists in handcuffs. You were able to sleep just a bit. Water was the only thing they occasionally gave you. Your wounds hurt constantly and whenever you moved the soldiers pointed their guns at you. As if you had any chance at all of escaping that nightmare.

You were relieved when at last the truck came to a stop. The desperation of having been shut up in that space for so many hours would end any minute now. You didn't understand that the ordeal could start up again: the spotlights, the prodding, the punches, the torture . . . now it was the military police's turn.

They too would have to open a file. They too would have their torturers.

This was no comparison to the previous episodes. You might even have thought, incredibly enough, that your body needed that treatment. Resigned more than frightened, you withstood the next torture session with the certainty that life was abandoning your body. You never thought of letting go completely, you preferred that they reveal, little by little, the path to your death. They know better than anyone when to stop, which string to pull, where to hit you, how to apply the electrical shocks, how to blind you with the light. You never thought that a marionette could take so much—there was always just a bit more to give, always something for the next session.

THE DAY FINALLY ARRIVED when you would be presented to the press. Without knowing when or where, all of a sudden you were in front of several cameras. Your *compañeros* were present as well, and other people who'd been tortured. You didn't recognize anyone. You were at the Attorney General's office, according to what they told you later. One way or another, everyone was afraid to hear their names and the accusations of what they had not done.

Twenty people had been arrested. Five women and fifteen men, would finally go before a judge to be tried for disturbing the peace. When each of you heard your name, you stepped forward to be photographed and to hear the charges against you. It was then that you learned the real names of those whose ideals you shared. The identities of the ghosts you had lived with were revealed.

Your name resounded in your ears. You tried to pretend you weren't there by keeping your head down, but the flashes exploded in your face.

"Conspiracy, forgery of documents, possession of military-grade firearms, association with criminals."

That's what you were accused of. At first you didn't understand anything. You only knew that your ideals were now jammed down your throat from so many blows. You were beginning to experience powerlessness and indignation as if they were every day realities—you even thought the name they called you wasn't yours. It was someone else's, not yours.

Several people with small notebooks didn't let a word of the statements slip by. "There are twenty of them; they're like copper;

by their looks, it's possible they have given in," you heard one of them say.

You weren't allowed to answer the reporters' first questions. You discovered a well-staged scene to your right with guns, bombs, documents and briefcases that supposedly belonged to all of you. You didn't recognize anything as yours or as belonging to any of your *compañeros*.

Finally the word came: your new residence would be Lecumberri, the ultra high-security prison. You were invited as a guest and you had no other option than to accept. As you were leaving, you looked into Dora's eyes and tried to wish her good luck. She was going to Santa Marta.

You never imagined word would spread so quickly. You had become so used to being incommunicado that it took you by surprise to learn that the day after your "presentation" to the media one of your daughters and your sister-in-law had come for a visit. You realized then that there had been no mistake, that your name was Miguel Ángel, and that the past you had hid so well was returning, along with the corresponding actors, in an untimely fashion. Strangely, you came to the realization that the past month of your life was related to the same person whose daughter was visiting him right now—the puppet had a name. It took you a while to recognize the two women. A feeling of peace came over you, a calmness when, in spite of what you looked like, the odor emanating from your body, your distant gaze, they recognized you. You were happy simply realizing that there could be life after death . . .

FEDERICO KNEW ALL THE STEPS by heart. Once the bus reached Avenida de Zarazoga, he would go to the bathroom in the back, take off one shoe and sock and, with a tightly folded piece of cardboard, he would hide the money in the sole of his foot. This way, when they frisked him, he put his foot on the floor and concealed the packet. The amount didn't vary much from visit to visit, but it was used for bribes or other unforeseen situations.

His nerves no longer got the best of him when the prison guard, a brusque woman, drew the curtain and began to check every inch of him. Federico knew his responsibilities and the ensuing consequences if the money didn't reach its destination.

Wednesday, Saturday and Sunday were the days Federico went with his mother to visit his father. The trips to Mexico City seemed to become part of a new way of life. They always came across news that weakened the emotional stability of the family.

Hallways, bars, faces, uniforms, noises, cells, workshops, newspapers, guns, the frights, the nerves, the shouts, barbed-wire fences, laughter, music, illusions, cries, anxiety, food, tension, helplessness, smells, whispers, the railings . . .

Everything that at one time had surprised him, all that had caused fear and insecurity, was now completely normal in a terrible way.

Federico soon learned that it was better to live with surprises, with the unexpected. Nothing shocked him anymore. The only certainty in life, as his father had repeated to him over and over again, was death. Everything else had a solution. The most important thing was to live each moment and not fall back into the past and make accusations. Even though it was futile, there would be time for that later. There were new rules to live by in prison. If you violated them you might regret it, but no one really knew what would happen if you did.

Federico was in sixth grade. He learned to play with the pleasure of inventing the stage around him. His schoolmates didn't understand why he missed so many days of school and, in spite of his strange situation, they never asked awkward questions. He continued his karate classes, he went to his English lessons with his great aunt, and he flirted with the girls in his class to try and get a kiss. In all actuality, though, he preferred to run away and leave it all to chance—and see whether the girl he liked would reward or reject him.

When they visited the prison, he knew by heart where every street vendor outside the gates was located. Every day he took mental note of who might be missing that day—maybe the man who sold the *jícama*, or the one who sold *tamales*, the woman who sold *atole*, or the one who sold the *cemita* sandwiches, or the family that rented women's clothing; as if all of these details were part of the visit's prerequisites. The two main entrances to Lecumberri were now familiar—the one for men, with its imposing door on Eduardo Molina, and the one for women around back. Federico learned how the system granted you an existence for a specific period of time. Nothing was left to chance. Destiny belonged in large measure to the decisions, to the people in power.

Human degradation was evident to Federico inside the prison. Precisely at his age, when one is about to lose the innocence of childhood, when nerves are confused with sexual awareness, Federico discovered that degradation every time he looked up to see the walls, to contemplate the number of lives that depended on watchtowers. Each person with his own story, his own horror and his every hope lost.

"This is the worst prison in the world," he had heard one of his father's cellmates say, and he felt almost proud. Few at his age had been to that wretched place, filled with insecurity, inequality, corruption, injustice. At that age, when you discover your own identity, when consciousness becomes the wall you put up against the world and everything becomes dubious, no authority figure can wear you out. Federico understood that he could begin to get used to the indignation and the powerlessness. However much he wanted things to be different, there was little he could do.

"Prison rips your soul out and kills all intelligence," he once read, understanding the meaning behind Martí's words.

Federico always stayed close to his mother. He felt he could protect her from anything, even when she appeared before the attorney who recognized the courage of this Mexican woman. She stood out in the group that came to denounce the irregularities of which their husbands, brothers and sons were victims.

"In Mexico there are no political prisoners." The orders continued as if the situation this husband-father was in didn't exist, as if the treatment he received from those who controlled the prison block didn't matter.

"It's official procedure, we're keeping our promises, resolving the problem, it's the unbreakable law . . ." that was what they heard every time one of those fat-assed civil servants opened their mouths regarding the protests of mistreatment of prisoners.

In spite of the past, in spite of the fact that he didn't confess that he had remarried a *compañera* in the organization, Federico's mother continued helping his father. The father, for his part, was fearful of being abandoned in that black palace.

Lawyers, bail, donations, journeys, cooking, greetings, interviews . . . Not even Federico's mother knew where she got the strength to do it all. The few times that the couple would discuss anything about their relationship, Federico understood just in time that he had to go find an opponent to play chess with. It was difficult to leave his father, but the circumstances warranted placing the pawns on another chessboard.

How does one explain the time, the needs, the rediscovery of life? How does one avoid the anguish that there won't be any appeals? How does one forget the abandonment? Words can't always communicate meaning, looks sometimes cannot be interpreted, and Federico hardly understood anything as he sat on the cement bench in the prison block, the sun beating down on his face. It's difficult to pick fights after two years and eight months.

Prison was a good way to study one's actions.

Having your feelings ache is worse than your physical self being torn apart. Federico understood routines, he didn't yet know about love, much less about the relationship between his so-called "parents." He was just barely beginning to pay for his own actions . . .

Morón was originally from Peru. He traveled through Uruguay until he got to Mexico, where he participated in the *Liga 23 de Septiembre*. He never considered himself defeated, in spite of being imprisoned in another country. He fought wherever he was, holding onto the ideal that all the countries in America were one. Wherever there were injustices there needed to be a fight, nothing else mattered.

His biggest dream was always to be transferred to the "M" block at Lecumberri, the one reserved for political prisoners. There, he thought that he would feel less overwhelmed by the desperation of being imprisoned.

His old man and lady, as he called them, didn't know anything about his whereabouts. He sent them letters telling them about Mexico. He invented imaginary friends and streets that he had never walked down.

When he arrived in Mexico he wasted no time in joining the guerrilla. He spent his days saying that life was too short to allow oneself the luxury of squandering it and not taking part in the fight. "Put up a fight" was his favorite saying. He figured that his time in prison would help prepare him for other matters of warfare, so that when he got out he could join yet another revolutionary movement.

You met him in the cell. From the moment you arrived at Lecumberri his persona gave you a good vibe, he was always attentive, he never complained. He didn't even complain about the mistreatments in prison.

Susceptibility is the mother of disputes. You knew that well,

particularly when many different guerrilla fighters were all together in the same prison. In there with you, aside from Morón,
there were three others from the *Liga 23 de Septiembre*, another
from your group, one from the *Lucio* group and one more from
the *Comandos Armados Revolucionarios del Pueblo*. The debates, the
ideological philosophies, the concepts, the tactics, the mecha-
nisms and strategies for taking control, they were all a constant
source of annoyance, even though you all shared the desolation
of prison. You seldom agreed when a disagreement arose.

Aside from the political prisoners, you also shared the cell
with seven common prisoners, who for the most part shied away
from any political or ideological commentaries.

Morón was always ready to take care of any need your family
might have or help with the visitors of any other *compañero*. His
friendliness provoked some jealousy on your part, as his attitude
won over the affections of your family.

One Sunday, your daughters arrived with breaded veal cutlets
to celebrate Morón's birthday. They knew it was his favorite dish.
It caused you great resentment, you were indignant arguing that
you and everyone else was in prison busting your balls, and they
show up to celebrate the Peruvian's birthday. You didn't
understand their behavior—you prisoners, fucked up there in
prison, knew that you could die at any moment.

Everyone looked on, understanding, pitying you from afar.

Perhaps Morón had a premonition and from the birthday on,
he started to constantly whistle a melody. It was the melody of a
song in which the character of the lyrics spent his time saying
goodbye to his neighbors, the seasons of the year, the sun, the
water.

That Wednesday you couldn't have felt more desolate. In the
early hours of the morning some of the members of the
commando met in your cell accompanied by Javier, the drug
trafficker with whom you had established a good relationship.

They called Morón and took him away. You couldn't go back to sleep, nor could any of your *compañeros*. It wasn't normal for the commandos to come for someone at 2:00 a.m., unless, like birds of prey, they arrived to announce a misfortune.

"*El Jefe* wants to chat."

That was the response that remained floating in the air in the face of the surprise, the anguish, the doubt, the panic of imagining the worst for Morón. A certain calm wanted to take hold of your state of mind. You hoped that since Javier the nark was involved nothing bad would happen.

Two hours later you were taken, along with the other political prisoners, to a cell completely bathed in blood—the ceiling was dripping with it as if the concrete itself were bleeding. You tried to interpret what Morón's fate, obvious now, had been.

You and the others cleaned the cell for an hour and a half. This is how you said goodbye to your exemplary *compañero*, the combatant from America, the tireless fighter. While you cleaned, mixing water with blood, you couldn't stand the silence, conscious that death was present in that room.

The powerlessness destroyed you, yet even your tears couldn't save you. Your wife and son arrived at the prison. You had forgotten that it was the day you yearned for with such longing, the day you would see your family. Now it would be difficult to face them and give them answers as to Morón's whereabouts.

"This fight is still in its infancy," was the only thing that came to mind to justify what had happened to Morón.

"Many will have to die before our objectives are met."

The sentences sounded hollow to you and they didn't console your family at all. On the contrary, you needed someone to take pity on you, to take you in his or her arms and drown the pain.

How to explain to them that one of the most valuable *compañeros* was no longer there? How to avoid the cries of desperation?

How to tell your family about the situation, so much like a nightmare? That you had cleaned the cell where Morón had ceased to exist? How to endure the visit now, what to say about death as it takes different shapes, colors, smells, images, and that in Lecumberri you see it all?

From that point on, at mealtime, you swallowed power-lessness, bitterness, breathlessness, and helplessness; little by little you began to understand that life indeed had a strange master . . .

WHAT A FUCKED-UP DAY. You never realize the intensity of danger until things happen, and when you gather your thoughts and remember the events, the images return and you realize what could have happened.

The hands and face of that prisoner remain etched in my memory.

Like any other day, Mama and I arrived at the prison. It was Wednesday. At the entrance we met the mother of another political prisoner who had been detained after Papa and who was in the same block. The woman's nickname was *Gamucita*, because she looked a lot like one of the characters in *The Burrón Family* comic.

We went through the routine formalities together: check points, searches, notes, requirements that were now familiar to us after five months of going to Lecumberri. Nothing seemed out of the ordinary. On the contrary, we thought everything was in its proper place.

We passed through the panoptic center of the prison structure recounting the latest family worries, which by now were routine.

We knew that when we got to the door of the block where our prisoners were, each of us would take a different route down the long hallway and enjoy the few minutes of the visit. They were usually so short that we never had enough time to fill Papa in on all the events, whether they had happened just recently or during the two years he was away.

When we reached the gated entrance to our block we sensed

that the usual familiarity was missing, a strange awareness filled the air. The three of us felt it but no one said anything. Maybe it was just that our nerves had gotten the best of us. The guard on watch wrote down the names of the prisoners we were visiting, he took the entrance passes and gave us the metallic number chips we had to turn in when we left. When we were about to enter the hallway and hear the names of the prisoners who had visitors called, we didn't notice Papa or Carlos among the blue uniforms. They were usually awaiting our arrival. Instead, a desperate cry stopped us from entering. A young man appeared amidst the curious prisoners who were crammed up against the bars. With a plea in his voice he warned us not to enter.

"They've been moved!"

He tried desperately to explain so we would believe him and thus not go into the block. His hands grabbed the bars and his panic so impressed us that even the policeman and the other prisoners were surprised. His words seemed unnecessary: his mere actions expressed what he wanted to say.

The police attendant, nervous, excused himself by saying he didn't know anything.

"They moved them last night, they aren't here anymore," the young man continued shouting.

Stupefied, the attendant proceeded to close the entrance which seconds before had been opened for us. He offered confused explanations regarding his ignorance of a possible move and checked his grimy booklet where all prisoner changes should have been registered.

"That seems right, they were moved last night," he commented as he turned around quickly in search of a superior for help. As soon as he said that, the face of the young man relaxed, his muscles appeared to return to their place, his hands no longer gripped the steel bars with such force. He had fulfilled his mission—the struggle had not been in vain.

A higher-ranking police guard arrived and the attendant explained the case. They reviewed the moldy booklet once again and sent for other lists to try and locate the whereabouts of our family members.

We couldn't shake the impact. When Mama tried to thank the young man for his message, he had already disappeared among the prisoners who were awaiting visits. His only mission had been to warn us. That was his intention.

The commotion grew, the situation made our imaginations run wild. Why had he warned us with such anguish? Who was he and how did he recognize us? Why hadn't they notified us about the move when we entered the prison? Why did they want us to go into a block where Papa no longer was? Who would have stopped that young man from warning us . . . ?

"Miguel Ángel was transferred to cell block 'A,' Carlos to 'I,'" was the answer.

We accompanied *Gamucita* to the gate of the cellblock where her son was. Then we walked the entire way back through the panoptic center to arrive at cellblock 'A.' The official who had accompanied us spoke to the attendant and they immediately yelled out Papa's name. They opened the gated entrance and motioned us toward the end of the hallway. Mama and I walked cautiously, and before we had gone thirty steps, a man ran out to meet us and took us by the arm, stopping us. It was Vicente, a *compañero* from Papa's organization. He had been detained at the same safe house.

He sat us down on one of the benches. The wildest thoughts imaginable started to race through my mind.

"It's better not to see him right now. He's on the cleaning shift, but if they see that someone has come to visit him they'll demand money. Everything you paid in 'G' block, so he wouldn't be bothered, doesn't matter here. If you see him now they will want to strip you of everything and that's not fair."

At first Mama and I didn't understand what Vicente was saying. He only wanted to protect us so the vicious cycle of "payments" wouldn't start up again.

"After a few weeks, when they realize that no one comes to visit him, they'll stop badgering him. The commando of this block is a bit more laid-back."

No one visited Vicente, so they could never force money from him. Even though he had had many problems at the beginning, little by little they had stopped bothering him. By that time, he had gained the confidence of several members of the commando and he was well respected in the block. He had started a literacy circle, among many other things.

We talked and talked. Vicente could calm anyone down, and in spite of the worries we felt about not seeing Papa, about not being close to him and talking with him, Vicente listened to what had happened to us. It was then that we realized what could have happened to Papa, and how, thanks to that young man, we were able to avoid it.

There was no difference between 'A' block and the others, the same faces were there, the same decor, the frustrations didn't change.

About an hour after we arrived, when we were a bit more relaxed, a hollow thud was heard all through the block. A few meters away, a child had slammed onto the cement hallway floor. He had been playing on the second floor while his parents enjoyed an intimate visit. He was climbing on the railing when he slipped. The floor was instantly bathed in blood.

The prisoners mingled about observing, but no one dared do anything. A tragedy of this proportion was capable of arousing all sorts of reactions. Once the initial impact was over, I tried to look at the body but Vicente, embracing me, forced me to look the other way. He knew the state I was in and he didn't want the scene to cause me any further anxiety.

Several police officers entered immediately and minutes later a stretcher and some nurses arrived. The mother was torn apart with grief, the father, pale, couldn't believe what he was seeing. Both of them had a guilty look on their faces. The body was taken away and the blood was immediately washed from the floor with power washers, the same kind they occasionally used to wake the prisoners at night and torture them psychologically. Things returned to "normal"—perhaps there were worse things to worry about.

The accident had made us extremely tense. I was relieved when I saw Papa walk towards us, bucket in hand, on his way to cleaning duty. His presence brought me back from the edge of a cliff, I felt safe again. When he saw us he pretended not to know us. He knew why Vicente had stopped us at the entrance. He was only able to turn his head as if he didn't care, and wink at me. That gesture said everything.

Vicente became somewhat uncomfortable when he saw Papa pass by. He hadn't had time to tell Papa why he was there, and he feared his reaction. Our conversation started up again as if nothing had happened, our nerves made the effort to return to their respective places.

The supposed calm was broken again by a sharp whistling sound that deafened the place. Several policemen made a sudden presence with billy clubs, blackjacks and even pistols. Everyone was in disbelief. Vicente once again quieted us and explained in a soft voice that it was most likely a drug snitch, even though we wondered what the police were doing there. In prison one never knew what could happen.

It wasn't so normal to have the police interrupt daily life in the prison block, more so during visiting hours. Everyone was on edge. Silence reigned in every centimeter of the hallway until the policemen cautiously took away two prisoners from one of the cells at the entrance, just where Papa was getting ready to mop.

"You'll see, it was only drugs," Vicente commented when it was all over.

It was two o'clock and the siren sounded, announcing the end of visiting hours. Perhaps Vicente was happy that they had transferred Papa, because he had time to talk to us. Before we left he gave us the necessary instructions to continue pretending to visit Papa until the commando stopped their attempts at extor-tion.

Near the exit, in the last hallway where matchboxes hung from thin threads, decorating the wall like the Wailing Wall, we found the pleas for alms for those who were in solitary confinement. We saw *Gamucita* again and she immediately told us about the difficult situation her son was in, exactly as Vicente had warned us. In Carlos' case it had started all over again.

The memory of that day is mixed with a variety of feelings. Mysteries still float in the air—reflecting back even today gives me goose bumps. The more time goes by the fewer answers there are—hands, blood, music, noise, grief, bodies, and faces. Tattoos in the distance. In Lecumberri the possibility of consoling or pitying those who challenged the government wasn't allowed. Surely that prisoner who had warned us had put his life at risk.

YOU LEAVE AFTER A VISIT to the prison and observe the thousands of people all over. You imagine that money can't be worth all that much, that its value is relative in comparison to such suffering, and now you have to get the bail together to obtain his freedom. How much could one hundred thousand pesos have been worth in 1974?

The math seemed simple enough to you, just like the many other times you imagined saving money for something. So, on a napkin next to a cup of coffee, you figured it all out.

If only every person you saw could give you one peso, one miserable shitty peso. Who can deny anyone a fucking peso? What does it take away from anyone to give you, as a gift, as alms, a frigging peso? Anyone can be moved by such a request.

You have many friends, tons of acquaintances.

One should help those who suffer because they tried, that asshole in jail, because . . .

You call, you solicit, you seek out, you set appointments, you let people know, you insist, you insist.

"But of course . . . "

"Count on me . . . "

"How couldn't I . . . "

"Friends understand . . . "

A long time friend of Papa's, Tlapopoca, with all the fanfare typical of him, took on the task of raising some of the bail money. He said that in no time he'd get the amount needed to get Papa out of jail.

After two months Mama and I went to his house to see how much he had raised. He invited us in . . .

"Take a guess, you can't imagine; let's see *señora*, how much do you think? What's more, even Borja, the player for the 'America' team, contributed. What do you say, how much do you think we raised, how much, let's see, how much do you think?"

His words inflated our illusions. His insistence, his triumphant attitude, the solution at hand, the satisfaction. It got to the point where I thought that my anxiety, which had become a way of life, had come to an end. With his promise, I believed in the possibility of seeing my father a free man. Shit, even Borja had helped out, so everything was resolved, wasn't it?

"You can't imagine, can you?"

A parade of numbers danced in our heads, but we didn't dare utter an amount.

"Ten thousand pesos!"

An explosive and recriminating "What?" resounded inside Mama and me; all those big words were for ten thousand shitty pesos. At this rate it would take 20 fucking months to get the one hundred thousand pesos we needed to see Papa free.

Mama appeared surprised. It's fine that no one gives money away, even one fucking despised peso that can get on anyone's nerves, but why such a freaking fuss for so little, why did he make such a big deal out of it? What was all the joking around and getting our hopes up so high for only ten percent of the bail? That was the amount that a friend of the family who regularly bet on cockfights had promised to give us once he paid off his debts.

A political prisoner isn't just anyone, even more so if he's a member of the guerrilla. To be involved with the family, to help out, that could get you in trouble. The leftist organizations warned about the danger of guns, of fundamentalism, and for that no one dared come near us.

Meanwhile, another *compadre* who was always against Papa's ideals immediately came to us and never failed with his two thousand pesos a month. The Jesuits, for their part, sent word to

Amnesty International about the case, and every day a priest would go to the prison with a meal for Papa.

It never fails. The people you think will be right up front always go to the nosebleed section, and watch what's going on from afar. Meanwhile, those you least imagined, those who weren't even on the list, buy a front-row seat, a reservation to support, to help out at precisely the right moment.

A SIGNATURE WE WERE ABLE to obtain after much pushing a
shoving was the safeguard that finally set Papa free from behir.
bars.

But to get that scribble to the bail bondsman was another
daring feat. The *Monumento a la Revolución* was practically on top of
us—we had walked by the fronton court more than ten times.
Even from the street you could hear the screams and applause for
the players that were battling it out inside. We couldn't find the
fucking bail bond agency *La Guardiana* anywhere. The numbers
on the buildings were hidden; we followed the lawyer's directions
step by step, always winding up at the same dead end. Each and
every one of our nerves was on edge. We felt as if the bail agents
could protect us from all possible evils, as if all the risks, the
torture and extortions, would end when we arrived at the agency
with the paperwork we needed to have signed.

Exhausted and desperate to find the address, Mama and I
stopped. It was quarter to seven at night, closing time. If we
didn't arrive on time we would slow down the procedure. They
were waiting for us, the lawyer had informed them to wait for us
with everything ready to finish the fucking paperwork. The running around never ended.

On one side of the fronton court, a building rose up with the
name and logotype of the lion that indicated the offices of the
bail bonders. We had been so anxious that we hadn't noticed it.
Our despair had blinded our hopes . . .

IT SEEMED LIKE the day would never arrive. You got ready early in the morning, and prayed even though you didn't believe in God. Your cellmates noticed something strange about you—only two of them knew why you were so nervous. There was no way that you would let anything, even the smallest detail, keep you in any longer.

You had said that you couldn't stand the nightmare any longer, the same old faces, the muscles cringing expecting to be hit, the imaginary line of farewells watching your family leave.

It was seven o'clock in the morning and already you wanted to go out to the patio, you wanted to walk, to run. The desire to tell everyone to go to hell was building, to tell them all that this would be your last day here as a distinguished guest. You couldn't leave the cell yet though, you had to repress those desires, the frustration. No one could know it was your last morning. The lawyer had finally gathered all the necessary requirements so the judge would let you out on bail.

You remembered cases where even at the last moment, some of the prisoners were never freed on the set day due to one excuse or another, or when the commandos created a situation that prevented the prisoner from reaching the street. They could "make" you sick, or beat you up even, just to say goodbye. After having fought for your life every minute in Lecumberri, the possibility of being killed still existed. It wasn't right that at this moment the smallest rash move could jeopardize everything. It was better to calm down and organize what you would do once you were free. You knew that two women were thinking about you—the mother of your children, she had helped you all this time—and the woman with whom you had shared your ideals during the last years of your clandestine life, your fight. She was still in jail.

You would have to look for work. You would run into those who had turned their backs on you, you would greet those who hadn't forgotten you.

What the hell would you do, how would you act once you were back on the street?

You sat in the corner of your cell with your face in your hands, you closed your eyes and more doubts filled your mind. You weren't sure how that family of yours, the one you had abandoned, would welcome you. Would you go to Puebla? Would they leave you now that you were free? Would your friends invite you out now that you had returned from the underground? What would your father think of you? It had been so long since he had visited you. How would you reorganize your life? Would you ever again see the people you were with in prison? The ones you had shared so many intense situations with. What would you find? The uncertainty, the doubt, the lack of clarity pierced everything.

Without meaning to, you woke up your cellmates. No one dared say anything. They left you alone in the corner. Those who knew the date, the specific day, maybe they wanted to switch places with you, be in your shoes, go in your stead knowing that it was one of the happiest and most difficult days of your life. The others just thought you were acting odd. Your behavior didn't bother them—maybe they understood why you were nervous.

At last the clock struck eight. Ever since you had opened your eyes at four that morning, time had seemed eternal. Never had you had such a torturous wait as this. Throughout your entire stay in prison those four hours were the worst. As you held onto your hopes it made you sick to think it could all vanish into thin air.

You managed to make it into the hallway, and saw how the cell doors were opening. You encountered the tired, bored, hopeless faces that looked up tediously. No one perceived that your hair was combed carefully as you made your way to the shower. Why was it that you had combed it before taking a shower? You were one of the first to reach the shower, if you could call those tubes hanging from the wall a shower. You enjoyed the cold water on your body as you had only a few times in your life. You stayed longer than usual under the running water. Once you were finished you left all your toiletries behind: soap, shampoo, the coarse loofah scrub brush, toothpaste, even the towel.

The clatter to get ready to line up for breakfast, plates in hand, was ceaseless; after that, everyone hurried to their cell doors. You followed with the sole thought of not letting them notice you. Truth be told, you had promised never to eat that food again, least of all on the day you would be freed. They might put something in it to make you sick, even poison you. Your nerves eliminated any inkling of hunger. You got your ration and you pretended to start eating, then went over to the sinks. You asked what time it was.

"Quarter to nine."

You imagined that at that very moment your family would be entering the court accompanied by the lawyer, who would have your file, the bail money, the verdict, the signatures, the official seals, even a certain amount of money for last-minute difficulties which could often delay the procedures.

You didn't know if anyone in your family would be coming to pick you up. You thought about the possibility that only the lawyer would be waiting for you. What would you say to him? The idea made you tremble, you felt like a child on the first day of school, and you thought back to the fear your children felt when they had let go of your hand, years ago. You barely made it to one of the cement benches to sit down and breathe deeply. You hoped to shake off your doubts by breathing in some air.

You had put up with the pressures for so long that you couldn't break now, not at the last moment. Once you recovered, you went back to your cell. You folded up your serapes like you had every day, you left the few articles of clothing you had in a pile on the mattress that had served as an escape, when you slept, from the nightmare you were living. You went over to the table where the games were kept, you bid farewell to the chess set, which had helped you feel engaged, as you had spent so much time with it. You took the wooden puzzle that made so many shapes that drove you crazy in your hands, the one that everyone had always asked to borrow. You caressed the deck of cards and took one last look at the dominos. Jail was the game of chance university, a way to kill time. You piled up the books you had read and read over again—it had been a while since they prohibited your family from bringing you any new ones.

Before leaving, you took a good look at the four walls and the ceiling of your cell. You swore at them, you loved them, you hoped to remember and forget them. And finally, making sure that no one would see, you spit on the iron-barred door that every night, with its unbearable squeaking, had shut from the outside. You put the packet of *Delicados* non-filter and the thin braided bracelet that Morón had given you in the pocket of your uniform. You left the matches in their place. Anyone could give you a light on the outside.

You thought you heard your name, your heart wanted to jump out of your chest. Your hands began to feel the sensation of thousands of ants marching and then drowning in the sweat that leaked out of every pore.

When you left your cell you thought that everyone was watching you and that they were going to scream out "Don't let him leave." You forced yourself to walk slowly, on the one hand as a safety measure and on the other to control the desire you had to run like crazy. You wanted to cross that imaginary line, arrive at the barred gates, pass through them. But that would have given you away. Every time you moved your legs they wanted to fly. You tried to clear your mind so that nothing would give you away. It was torture to discover what every prisoner felt at that moment, to know that the *comandante* knew you would be free that day. The hallway went on forever, your steps became endless on the way to the exit. You didn't even have time to go back to say goodbye to those whom you wanted to thank even just a bit.

Fifty meters from the exit a prisoner came up to you. You stopped in your tracks and your eyes clouded over.

"They've been calling your name from the court for fifteen minutes, hurry up, brother."

You almost didn't hear him, but it served as an excuse for you to pick up the pace and end that ordeal.

You arrived at the barred gate and the police attendant asked for your name. He still had the luxury of scolding you because they had been calling your name for some time. You didn't bat an eye. Instead you thought you would faint when you realized they were sending for you from the courtroom. You couldn't believe it; you had longed for that moment and now you couldn't believe it was happening. You signed your name next to the typed misspelling of it, and for the first time you didn't care how it was spelled. Your signature, after all that had happened, came out odd because of the trembling. You passed through the first barred gate and wanted to turn around before entering the central panoptic area to take one last look: your life, the world, the memories, the ideology, the sentiments. You took out a cigarette and asked the guard for a light.

You didn't know how to describe what goodbyes meant to you. You had once heard someone say that all goodbyes are sad, but on this occasion it was quite different. You tried to remember the important moments of your stay in prison—the emotions of your family arriving for a visit, the moments of terror and anguish. You walked alongside the guard without talking, you moved through the hallways that would "supposedly" take you to freedom. Everything was still relative, especially after spending six months and twenty-four days locked up in Lecumberri. What would happen if things didn't work in your favor and you had to go back to the cellblock like you had so many times before? As hard as you tried to keep a blank look on your face, to not give your thoughts freedom to fly around, the images and the fears returned. You wanted to wake up and pretend that nothing had happened, that you had no reason to say goodbye to prison. You didn't feel the least bit of compassion for those with whom you had shared miseries and misfortunes.

You thought back to when you passed over to the underground and the reflection pierced your soul.

At the first gated checkpoint they frisked every inch of you. You knew by heart the guard's maneuvers as he searched your body for strange objects. You had imagined this day so many times, and now it was becoming a reality. You filled out the form to gain access to the courtroom—your hands had recovered a feigned normalcy. You wrote your full name, the name of your lawyer, the date.

You walked through the never-ending hallways lined with archivists, smirking public servants who saw you as fodder for the sharks. You observed the trusty prisoners who were cleaning the offices, and with a look of solidarity their attitude of having a status of privilege for being the chosen ones, disappeared. Their demeanor was more like the longing to regain the lost chance of their freedom.

"It's not going to be easy. When you're in the street you'll know why I'm saying this. It's like being born again without a mother, without recognizing the world that you previously held in your hands."

The words of your drug-trafficker friend weighed more

heavily than ever. Now you understood what he meant, you knew that hopefully you would soon be in the street next to other people, with cars, construction, the city . . .

At the second and last checkpoint, the guard in charge scolded you for not having your garrison cap on. No one had noticed that oversight, not even you, who had thought about and studied every last detail. Your state of nerves had been such that you had overlooked that routine detail. The cap had almost grown roots in your hair, but now you weren't wearing it.

You were terrified they would take you back to your cell. The rules stated that every prisoner who appeared in court had to be dressed to perfection in uniform. You weren't even sorry; it was your own fault. You assumed responsibility. You apologized softly, and without knowing why the guard took a liking to you.

"Listen, you," he said authoritatively to one of the inmates cleaning the offices. "Lend this guy your cap. When you come back you can return it to him, but don't let it happen again."

You felt like hugging him, thanking his blessed mother for that small gesture.

Confused, the prisoner obeyed the order. It wasn't common for a guard to behave like that. In general they made prisoners return to their cells for whatever they were missing, making them run the risk of losing their turn in court and burying the case. If you didn't appear at the right time after being called, they continued on with the next case and you logically lost that opportunity until further notice, having to go through, of course, additional formalities.

You took the cap, thanked him with a nod of your head and a silent "gracias," and staring at the police guard you continued on, knowing that you would never return that piece of the uniform.

When you finally arrived at the courtroom they sat you down next to a desk. You imagined that your lawyer and some family members, if they had decided to come for you, would be in the office next door.

No one looked at you—you were simply an object. You didn't have feelings. To those pencil pushers you weren't worth anything. It didn't matter that for you this was one of the most important days of your life. For them your case was just one more part of their boring daily routines, slow, degrading, cancerous. They had seen this so many times: the same faces of hope, the nervous attitudes, the uneasiness of observing how lives slipped away during the procedures, the despair of time drowned.

They only looked at you to determine the possibility of blackmail in your eyes—a bribe—to pad their miserable salaries.

You sat and waited there for over three hours. You didn't speak; you withstood the pressure. In spite of the tremendous desire to smoke you didn't even light a cigarette because you might bother someone. You observed the daily routine of the office. People coming and going from one place to another, the employees flirting amongst themselves, the devouring of sweets and sodas, the filing of nails, the amusing reading of comic books.

You carefully watched the parading of several men with piles of papers in their hands, the cases, the lives of an indeterminate number of jailed men that weren't important to anyone. The idea of your own case, and that of those around you became apparent. You reflected on the concrete life of your children. It was one thing to have them come visit you in prison and another entirely different thing to see them in their environment, in the house that was no longer yours. You recalled each one of them not by their names, not by their personalities. Instead, you referred to the phrases that each one coined when they were young: "*Te cusho con papá yoya . . . meeeno,*" for your eldest daughter. "*Anone me coto,*" for the next. "*Ateshion pasajeros abordar el avión,*" for the first of the male children. "*Se hace de día, se hace de noche,*" for the second boy. By reference only and thanks to a short visit to Lecumberri, you knew that the phrase of your last child was: "*Quen me lalo.*"

From time to time some guy with a pistol passed in front of you and you remembered your arrest. You had lived through so much since they had ratted on you—the police attack, the general paralysis that had stopped you from destroying the information, the fall of your other *compañeros*, the torture, the isolation, the transfer, being presented to the media, the declarations, the trial, your encounter with the family you had abandoned, the laments, the extortion, the injustice, the commandos, the drugs, the prostitution, the assassinations. Now that all this appeared to be over . . . you wondered what would be next.

At last you heard your name. You stood up without knowing what to do. You even thought that perhaps they were calling you to go back to the cellblock. They took you to another office where a secretary in a bad mood started to interrogate you while she typed. You tried to concentrate on the answers—God forbid she would become more irate than she already was. Your voice hardly came out of your mouth, that's how tense it was. When the young woman finished filling out the form she stood up without saying anything and left you there. Another hour had been eaten up. By that time your stomach was empty and you felt faint, you were exhausted. They called you again, you walked toward the person who had announced your name, and he gave you several papers indicating where you had to sign. You were about to sign when you realized you had no idea what those documents were. You remembered the advice, almost the law, of your lawyer, to not sign anything if you didn't know what it was. When you started to read the information the man with the squeaky voice became angry. You felt his disapproval, so you quickly glanced between the lines. No way could you piss off another vengeful public servant, even though it was your right to do what you were doing. You signed.

"This way," they said in exchange and the man took you to a large office filled with archivists and thousands of desks. There were people all around. At the other end of the room you discovered your lawyer's face, who with his hand up in the air, was signaling to you. At that moment you didn't see your daughter and your sister-in-law who were by his side. When you saw them, your eyes filled with a salty liquid, you had forgotten that sensation of consolation. Timidly you raised your hand while they ordered you to sit down on the bench to your right in front of a concert of typewriters. You shared the bench with several other prisoners. They all seemed to be feeling the same way. No one dared say a thing. With your glances you wished each other whatever luck you had left. Little by little they were calling the others' names; they took their belongings from under the bench.

When your turn came, someone asked you if you wanted to go back to the block for your things. The mere idea frightened you and you just shook your head, indicating "no."

You choked on your words and couldn't talk. One of the clerks gave you a suit that your daughter had brought so you could change your clothes. They escorted you to the bathroom. You changed, feeling clumsy and odd in front of the jealous look of the office worker. Once you had changed you didn't know what to do with the uniform. It occurred to you to ask the clerk to return the cap to its owner, but it seemed ridiculous. You rolled up the uniform and hugged it. Without a doubt it was your past.

It was three o'clock and the working day at the courtroom was coming to a close. Right in front of your eyes, filing cabinets that held decisions regarding the lives of men and women were being shut. The employees smiled now for any old reason. You ventured to take out a cigarette and ask the man accompanying you for a light. The first puff made you sick, your stomach was empty and you noticed how bad the smoke made you feel.

At the other end of the office, behind the immense counter, hands were waving at you. It was your lawyer who was motioning you to come over. You felt like a frightened animal—you didn't know what to do or if you had to ask permission to do it. Would they scold you if you approached the counter? You let inertia take over and you walked through the office. When you were standing in front of your daughter and your sister-in-law you broke down and cried like a baby.

The embrace was uncomfortable because of the counter. Your lawyer invited you to come over to the other side. You couldn't speak, the words wouldn't come out and you didn't move because no one had told you to. You ignored the fact that everything was in order, everything was over and everything was beginning anew that moment. All the official stamps and seals were there, the bribes had been distributed, all the signatures were in their respective places. The piece of paper your lawyer had in his hand was your ticket to freedom. You were free and no one had told you. Maybe you had imagined this moment, as if it were a movie and someone said your name and then a voice shouted "outside with you and beat it." But no, they had ignored you in spite of the fact that you were free to go. Then: go behind the counter, hug your daughter tightly, thank your sister-in-law, yank the paper out of your lawyer's hand and run away from there.

THE FOUR O'CLOCK SUN splashed across your face. Your daughter couldn't stop hugging you; she was telling you things you didn't understand. The street seemed strange, and the traffic startled you. Just before getting into your lawyer's car, your sister-in-law pointed out that you still had your wrinkled uniform under your arm. Just minutes before it hadn't bothered you. Your "old" skin was now ripped off, so you threw it into a trash can close to the car. You hadn't returned the cap—the guy who gave it to you would have to buy another one. You decided to keep it and put it in a bag.

The emotions were many. Free at last. You wanted to shout it out, so that all of Mexico City could hear you. You wanted to laugh your head off, jump all through the park in front of the prison, roll through the grass, do somersaults.

"Let's get something to eat," your lawyer suggested. You felt like inviting them to lunch, taking them to the best restaurant, drinking until you passed out. The happiness you felt was too big for you—you didn't know where to put it, what to do with it, how to act. Your mind appeared to be clear.

Every question they asked you answered incoherently, you felt like life was yours again, you felt like a newborn who was reemerging from the womb at forty.

After eating lunch in a restaurant close to the Puebla bus station, your daughter said the words you had so longed to hear.

"Let's go, they're waiting for us in Puebla." Your doubts vanished. In spite of everything, your family wasn't abandoning you.

You didn't know what to say when it was time to bid farewell to the lawyer. The words piled up in your mouth and you felt an infinite gratitude. He had made so many things possible. He had supported you and your family. He understood how you were feeling; he hugged you and asked you to call him the following week.

You began to feel uncomfortable. Your sister-in-law paid for everything, you felt defenseless and ridiculous in a world that you thought you had forgotten. Desolation came across your face and you couldn't find anything to talk about. When you boarded the bus they let you sit alone so you could gather your thoughts. It was a lot for such a short time.

Silent, you were grateful for that gesture—at last they understood what you were going through.

You leaned your head on the window and marveled at the road that would take you to Puebla. In prison you were convinced that not even your dreams were free—at times, when you dreamt, you experienced a strange pleasure that the nightmare was reality. You were sure about one thing—life would always be full of surprises.

I THINK I WAS WATCHING television that day. The world soccer cup was on, but other than seeing Papa come home, nothing really mattered. It was supposedly the day we were waiting for, the day he would finally get out of prison. They would stop bothering him and the trips to Mexico City would end. On the screen the players fought for the ball, but I was only watching in order to distract myself and stop thinking about tragedies. Everyone in the house was sitting on pins and needles.

"What if something was missing?"

"What if they don't let him out?"

"They're never going to hit him again."

"I hope all the documents are in order."

"I hope Adriana and my aunt arrived on time . . . "

My mind was bursting with fear. I wanted to push it to one side with the game between Holland and Argentina. I wanted to understand the chances each team had for playing in the semifinals, and how the idols Beckenbaur of Germany and Lato of Poland were shaping the international news stories with their plays, their goals.

An adolescent waiting around usually means trouble. More so on a day like that with all the anxiety, the memories, the hope. The minutes seemed to stand still; the clock was wearing out from looking at it so much.

At seven o'clock that night Mama sent me out to buy bread. The chore seemed absurd to me as I didn't want to move until we had some news. There were two blocks between the bakery and our house—I would be back in less than fifteen minutes, but my feelings paralyzed me. I accepted the task half-heartedly, yet before leaving I pocketed the jack knife that made me feel safe from a possible attack from the kids in the neighborhood. I didn't get along with them and we fought over any old thing. I wasn't very good at fighting, despite years of practicing karate.

The bakery was packed. With a frown, I took my place in line, hoping that the "gossiping señoritas" wouldn't take long.

When I arrived home, Mama didn't respond to my knocking. She was in her bedroom with my aunt and my sister Adriana, who had just arrived from Mexico City. When I saw them I didn't see any emotions on their faces, they were whispering.

"OK!"

"Finally!"

"He couldn't?"

I thought the worst when I saw them all consumed. Between the nervousness, the happiness and the affliction, it seemed like their reply took forever.

"He's taking a shower," Mama said, interpreting my torment.

Suddenly I had a great urge to urinate. There was no time to lose, I had to see him with my own eyes, to know he was real and that everything was over. My heart would never again be on the verge of falling off a cliff. Having him here with us seemed impossible, even if it were only for a few days. We would all carry on with our lives, by his side, as if nothing had ever happened.

I went slowly towards the bathroom—my steps seemed endless.

Could I interrupt his shower? I needed to see him outside of Lecumberri. Back home again, after so many years, so much longing, so many sleepless nights, such wear and tear, muscles contracted for so long. It seemed like there was no other way to be at ease with myself.

"Who's there?" he asked from behind the plastic shower curtain.

"It's me." My answer was muffled between the noise of the

running water and my urine in the toilet bowl. He stuck his head out. It seemed like he couldn't believe it, just like me. How was it possible that he was taking a shower at home? He felt odd, uncomfortable. It wasn't Papa, it was a stranger, a visitor, a friend of the family who was allowed to take a shower and spend a few days with us until he could get situated, find a job.

My eyes weren't lying. He was here, he had finally left the nightmare behind, and I wanted to throw myself into his arms.

"How are you?" was the question that stopped me from getting into the shower fully dressed to give him a kiss, even though men don't kiss, as he had once told David by mistake. I wanted to hug him, touch him, know that he was real.

"I needed to see you." As I said that, I discovered the scars from the torture, the marks left from the interrogations, the tattoos of the system. The look on my face made him feel even worse; he wanted to close the curtain. I wanted to protect him, make him feel comfortable, tell him not to be afraid, that he wasn't in danger, that I would fight off the neighborhood kids and their gang, just like I could fight off everyone who had mistreated him. That I was a green belt in karate, and he, instead of my father, could be my son. That I was there, ready so that nothing would happen to him. That his ideals had truly been worth going through such shit. That in the long run, the abandonment didn't matter for shit, that we would face the debts and that the family had taken him back without asking for anything in return. The most important thing was for him to stop feeling obliged, emotionally indebted. Life was just that—water running through pipes that didn't stop to question anything. We stared at each other for a few seconds, saying so much to each other. I think we even mutually admired each other. Instead of running to get wet by his side I flushed the toilet so my urine would disappear.

"I'll wait for you outside."

How long had it been since he had taken a hot shower? How would his body react? I left so he could enjoy it, and went immediately back to Mama's bedroom, where the whispering was still going on.

She didn't know how to react either, how to treat him, what to offer him. Maybe it was easier to visit him in Lecumberri. I suppose that the love she felt for him, even after so many years, still inhabited some space—her house, her mind, her nerves, her body.

At last our battle had ended: the trips to Mexico City, the long lines asking for help, the search for cash, the doors slammed in our faces, staying at our godparents' house, the squeaking of the security gates, the smell of cheap deodorant on the Mexico City/Puebla bus route, the powerlessness in front of the burocracy, the accosting of the commandos, the bad news, the subway stations packed with passengers, fending off hunger with tacos, the money hidden on the soles of feet, the interrogations before the prison visits, the stiff necks from dozing off on the bus, the inquisitive looks from the people in Puebla, the sad walks down *Avenida de la Reforma*, the *Monumento a la Revolución* with the emblem of the PRI and the bail bond agency off to one side, waiting rooms with authority figures, the alarming news in the press, the consoling pats on the back . . .

Papa is home with us, and we think that life continues.

Part 3

WE THINK THAT
LIFE CONTINUES

I was used to living with a ghost as my paternal image, with sporadic appearances that changed according to which day it was. But being face to face with Papa once again provoked a different type of expectation.

The fact that he hadn't seen the transformation from our childhood to adolescence robbed us, from time to time, of the bridge between us. At times we felt like strangers and so we were careful around each other. Puebla wasn't the place for him, he felt uncomfortable. Fifteen days after he got out he decided to return to Mexico City. That was why, Irving, your ghost lasted such a short time.

They suggested that I spend time with him during my school vacation, and also suggested the possibility of my going to live with him.

It was an exciting three weeks. I thought it was fascinating that he paid attention to me—he prepared my meals and was attentive to all my needs. We lived in an apartment that one of his aunts had lent him. In the mornings he looked for work and searched for old friends. I stayed at home to play with the grandchildren of that aunt, who lived across the hall from us. They were the classic cousins that you don't know you have, but that one day show up in your life.

Now and then he didn't come home for lunch, which turned me into a forced guest at the home of my new relatives. In the afternoons Papa and I set a goal to play ten games of chess, and the winner was whoever had more checkmates that day. We kept score on a daily basis and talked about everything we hadn't been able to until then. He told me about wet dreams, and from that moment on I waited impatiently. They were good times. During those days I had the ideal father.

On the weekends we visited the family in Puebla. We took the bus on Friday afternoon and returned Sunday night. Mama was apprehensive of the emotions that came over me while I was living with Papa. She was conscious of the fact that some moments can't be relived, that things can't go on as if nothing had ever happened, that being reunited could change at any given moment, and that what we hoped for as eternal happiness was impossible.

On the Thursday of the third week we had been living together, Papa came home later than usual. Fear overtook me and so many worries began to overwhelm me—it hadn't been long since he'd left Lecumberri. He arrived around nine o'clock at night, he had a somewhat afflicted look on his face and he asked me if we could talk. I knew, one way or another, that eventually we would have to talk about Dora, his *compañera* while he lived underground. She would be getting out of Santa Martha the following Monday, and Papa had made the decision to return to her side. He struggled with his words; he was uncomfortable when he asked me to take the time to consider if I wanted to live with him and Dora or if I would return to Puebla. Until that day when his determination became obvious, I had never before thought about the separation of my parents as a couple. We were quiet for a long time, yet, I think it was more difficult for him to stand the silence. I suggested that I think about it over the weekend in Puebla. I believe he was relieved. That evening, our chess games ended.

In Puebla I talked to Mama about the situation. She, more than anyone, knew that this day was bound to come; it was for that reason that she was wary about my recent emotions. She thought that I might not understand what could happen. There was no turning the page though—the following Sunday Papa went back to Mexico City alone.

It was good to reconnect with my lost father during those three weeks. We knew we weren't the same. We were a different father and a different son after such a long time. We had to reprogram ourselves; we couldn't erase the past. We had to overcome it in order to maintain the bridge—after all, life couldn't continue to be an obstacle for either one of us.

YOU ARRIVED THAT WEEKEND to visit us in Puebla. You were still acting strange. This was and wasn't your family—you really only visited us so you wouldn't feel guilty.

That Friday night when you arrived we were all celebrating. Adriana, your oldest daughter, was graduating from medical school. Many people had been invited to the party. You thought it was a bad time to arrive, as it was uncomfortable seeing so many old friends of the family. You hadn't had the opportunity to see them since you'd left prison. You had no alternative now—you met them all at your family's home, ready to go out and celebrate the occasion.

Since no one had expected you that weekend, you found the appropriate pretext to free yourself from your guilty feelings.

"Are you coming with us, Papa?" Adriana asked.

"No, go on ahead, have fun, I'll stay here with your brothers."

It was an easy way out. Why make the situation worse when you weren't even included in the plans for the party? Those celebrations had always made you feel uncomfortable.

It was a race to the finish: the different perfumes, the twenty odd people fighting for the bathroom, running each other over getting dressed and ready for the celebration. At around ten o'clock that night they had all gone and at last everything was calm. The house was turned upside down.

Your youngest son fell asleep immediately and you decided to play chess with the eldest, as you had in the past. You sat in the dining room and set up the board.

Half an hour later, the board covered with pawns, horses, a rook or two, a castle, a bishop, you were startled when you heard a strange noise. Your son thought it was normal, the house had its own noises.

"The neighbor's cats are always in the courtyard."

You weren't convinced. The fright took you back to the time, when in just one breath, life seemed to forget you existed.

It was your turn but it took you a while to move—you had lost your concentration. Your son sensed your discomfort, he started to talk to distract you but a second noise alarmed you even more. You had very clearly heard someone moving around on the grass in the courtyard. It could be the police again. They had followed you some days ago. This upset you greatly—you didn't know if they would arrest you again, if they would ask you for money, if they would torture you again. The thought of going back to prison was a permanent source of anxiety.

You wanted to control yourself and not alarm your son. You pretended to be calm after listening to the explanations that he managed with perfect self-confidence. The third time you heard something you couldn't bear it. Panic stricken, you checked every room, you went to the window that looked out to the street but you didn't see anyone. Your son became frightened. He didn't understand why you were so frantic; the different noises seemed normal to him. You confessed that the police had been following you for a while, somewhat to justify your incomprehensible behavior.

The persistent noise made you lose control. You had a dreadful feeling in your stomach. The horror of imagining yourself as a "guest" at Lecumberri once again took over. You went to the window that looked out over the courtyard and supposedly you discovered some men who were watching the house. The panic of thinking that those men were there for you made you want to run away. If you controlled yourself it was for your children.

You made the decision to leave the house. You covered your

youngest son with a serape and left the lights on in the dining room and in the kitchen. If they were on, no one would suspect anything. Hidden by the darkness, you took to the street through the garage door. You had to think about all the necessary precautions as you had two of your children with you.

You walked on looking for a taxi. At last, two blocks later, one appeared and you asked to be taken to the Santa María district. Your father's house would be a good place to spend the night. You needed security. You turned around constantly to make sure that no one was following the taxi. You had escaped the *vigilancia*, the supposed hunt.

The youngest of your sons didn't know where you were going. He was half asleep, uncomfortable, and he moved around from time to time. You were scared shitless, your body was shaking, the driver noticed and immediately he accelerated.

At a corner, thanks to the reflexes of the driver, you just missed hitting another taxi that had run a red light. The tension grew. You were desperate, your children were bothering you, you imagined what the people pursuing you could do if they caught you.

Your father's house was at the end of the street and you thought you had reached safety . . .

The large black door rose up in front of you like a wall. You rang the bell insistently while you held your son, asleep in your arms. No one answered. Your other son was knocking on the door and causing a racket. You switched your young son from one arm to the other, on the one hand due to the heat of his body and on the other because of the excitement. You feared that they had followed you unsuspectingly and that they would surprise you in the middle of the street. No one answered the knocking and ringing, not a single light gave the slightest indication that anyone was prepared to open the door. You began to shout; the neighbors heard you but not your half-brothers.

You were there for a long time, knocking desperately. There was no answer. You decided to return home as there was nothing else you could do, nowhere else to go. Once again you walked in the company of your children looking for another taxi to take you back. Along with the anxiety provoked by the noises and possible spies, you felt that the street was not safe.

You walked several blocks through Santa María, the tracks of your childhood, the neighborhood of memory. You knew the danger of those streets, the possibility of being held up. The tension grew. At last, when you reached the Bulevar de San Francisco a cab stopped. For a moment you felt comforted—it hurt not being able to protect your children. You thought they were more helpless than you yourself were.

You entered through the garage once again and the house was exactly how you had left it. The so-called men who were following you didn't make any movements that caught your attention. You put your youngest son in bed and invited the other one to get into a different bed with you. You wanted them near you. You had accepted the responsibility of being by their side. You couldn't sleep, you were nervous, even exhausted from all the excitement. You waited expectantly in case you heard something else. Perhaps it was your ghosts that kept you alert; they brought you back to the nightmare. What was so difficult to accept was that: there was no escaping them.

YOU DECIDED TO LOOK OVER the newspapers you had kept from when you were detained. There you were in a photo and you didn't even recognize yourself, maybe because of your busted up face or maybe because you didn't know if at that moment you were the man from the underground or the one who had broken away from his family.

The press' version of the story made you sad, the way the events were recounted. The newspapers said whatever they wanted, with the help of the "official" versions, but you understood that only you and the torturers knew the truth.

Your distress disappeared when you found out . . .

JANUARY: Go back to a normal life? What is normal? The days of a happy family, the time in the underground? They've busted my balls.

FEBRUARY: It seems like this could be the month of the family tragedy. My father, desperate, called me at the office. After talking with him I learned of an irreparable fact: my sister Julia had died in combat in Tabasco.

No scream can help, no cry can come out. My disgrace seems childish compared to this news.

And to think that I was afraid, when this month began, of the possible memories that would assail me.

There's no way to get rid of this pain. I can put up with the demented torture, but not this.

Julia, you were brave.

AUGUST: I had decided not to write in this notebook again. I feel fortunate to have time to work and carry on with my life, but even still, the police insist on leaving their personal mark.

"How many times have you seen death up close?" one of my sons asked me the other day. I didn't know how to count them: when I was detained, the never-ending rounds of torture; when the bullets whizzed by me that day they took me as a human shield to apprehend other *compañeros* in Nepantla; when I was in jail. How many times? Is it worth counting? Will we know when we are going to die? Is it worth anything?

DECEMBER AGAIN: Close to the 24th my old man abandons me; why do I say "abandons me," as if I myself have never done that?

"He's left us," is the only thing I could think to tell one of my children.

The old man had guts! The things I learned from him. On one occasion he commented that he felt responsible for Julia and me joining the guerrilla. I didn't have the nerve to tell him that decisions in life are independent, maybe irresponsible, and the only person that makes them is you yourself.

SOME TIME AFTER THAT, between dreadful bouts of agony (as Paul Anka would say, "The end is near . . . "), but not without living as he should have lived, my grandfather, my father's father, after announcing that he would "teach his biology classes at the university by means of the ouiji board," closed his eyes forever.

At four o'clock in the afternoon I had the opportunity to say goodbye to him. I think he recovered consciousness for a moment and he knew who was with him. People of all sorts were milling around at the door to his hospital room: ex-students, patients, friends, family members. The man of legends was becoming a man of flesh and blood—the one who challenged all means of authority, the one of the thousand and one anecdotes, the one who cured venereal diseases in both cultured citizens and the sinners of Puebla, the one of unimaginable adventures—the communist.

When I was alone with him, I thanked him silently for being a substitute for a time, for the father figure that I had so lacked. Such little time was left; his jokes were coming to an end, the tales, his after-dinner story telling, the didactic explanations of all sorts of things, the bets, his presence.

I leaned over to kiss his forehead and his sweat impregnated my lips. We all knew it was a question of minutes, maybe hours, but no one dared tell him, perhaps so as not to frighten away hope. I recall looking down at him from the head of that hospital bed. Grandfather dictated something to Aute that he would later tell us: "Tell me something ridiculous when my time comes."

I returned home to wait for Papa and Adriana, who were coming from Mexico City. Grandfather stayed in the hospital telling everyone to go to hell. At seven o'clock that night, when they arrived, it was too late. They hadn't had the opportunity to say goodbye.

At the burial I understood Papa. It seemed strange that a relationship existed between the body that we were saying goodbye to and the man who was hugging me off to one side, trying to console me. How old does one have to be to cry for the dead?

My father had a father and at that instant, we were both saying goodbye to him. I never knew what Papa thought about his own fatherly figure, because he never had the time to say goodbye to him. That regrettable circumstance seemed to be one of Papa's habits.

With my grandfather gone, I thought more about Papa; in spite of everything we were all in the same boat anyway. In practice, grandfather always wanted to teach us that life existed for one thing only—to live it.

How many times do we smell death? And birth?

Every day you woke up recounting the times you could have ceased to exist. When you were ten years old, for example, when that car flipped over precisely where you were walking.

From that incident on there didn't seem to be another until you decided to join the armed resistance, the clandestine movement. During training they always stressed the dangers that a guerrilla fighter faces, the wager with death, the probabilities of handing your life over in combat.

The day of your detention you knew that everything was over, but in one way or another you dodged those horrible days of torture until they took you to Nepantla to arrest some of your compañeros. It was there that you felt more than ever the brush with death: bullets whizzing by your ears—you and your *compañeros* were the police shield. They positioned you up front so the inhabitants of the safe house would stop shooting, so no officer would be wounded. You shouted to them to hold their fire, as they could hit you or one of your *compañeros*, but they didn't care.

Several *compañeros* fell that day, but once again you were spared.

Perhaps because of that you learned to enjoy every little thing: a cigarette, the countryside, the street, a couple drinks, the little money you had, your children.

You didn't know the exact date, but you knew the day would arrive.

THE TELEPHONE RANG. At times you want news to arrive at the right moment, as if that's possible. It was a Saturday just like any other—Mama was taking a shower, David and Adriana had gone out, you refused to wake up from your dreams, María was sweeping the house.

I picked up the phone. The voice on the other end sounded cautious. I asked who it was. I imagined that the person was desperate; they had to speak quickly and hang up, they had to deliver the blow softly. They asked me to get Mama. It was someone from the office where Papa worked. They told me as well that Papa had suffered an accident.

I ran to the bathroom. Between the noise of the shower and my urgency to speak, Mama didn't understand a thing I was saying. I barely heard her mumble she would be right out.

When I returned to the bedroom I discovered María shouting into the telephone, as if she knew something about the call. Her attitude surprised me—I had heard that Papa had had an accident and I imagined that the message wasn't all that bad, but María was uncontrollable.

Mama arrived behind me wrapped in a towel, dripping water all over the place. She grabbed the phone from María and readied herself for the news. Her face hardened. She didn't make the least of gestures, she shook her head up and down, as if the person on the other end could see her. She asked for a pen and paper, which I quickly got for her. María, at that point, was face down on the bed crying.

"Your father has had an accident," she repeated what they had told her. "You have to find your brothers and sisters." That was her last order, while, with forced steps, she got dressed and started making a series of phone calls.

I told Adriana and David to come home immediately. Everything pointed to a trip to Mexico City. I got you dressed and Mama told me to take you to Uncle Héctor's house. Her intention was for me to stay in Puebla as well, but I demanded to go with everyone else to find out what was happening.

When I left the house to take you to our aunt and uncles', I never imagined that two days later I would be walking down that same street with Papa in front of us.

They were waiting at the door. I barely said hello, I had to return home and leave for Mexico City as soon as possible. In less than an hour everything was ready. We were going in two different cars.

When we reached the first tollbooth in San Martín Texmelucan, one of the cars broke down so we all had to continue the trip in the other one. Even so, we managed to get comfortable. David and Adriana's boyfriend stayed behind, trying to fix the car.

We made the trip in silence. When we reached the second tollbooth, my aunt bought the newspaper *Últimas Noticias*, but she didn't have time to read it because Mama asked for it right away. She leafed through the paper and self-confidently said there was nothing about the accident. She had already found the article; she had seen it out of the corner of her eye. It was the first bit of information published about the assassination of Papa, attributing his death to a supposed marital dispute. Mama hid the paper. We insisted on taking a look, but she said that if we read in the car we would get sick. She put it behind her back and didn't let any of us have it. In this way we all continued to hope, except for Mama, who held back the desire to let it all out.

When we reached Mexico City we went to the Venustiano Carranza Police Station, where supposedly the voice of the mysterious phone call had told us we would find Papa.

A classic pencil pusher told us, so very calmly, as if he were referring to an object, that the cadaver was at the Benito Juárez Station. We lost all hope with those words: we had found out that Papa had died. At first you refuse to believe it. You don't understand, or you don't want to understand what the civil servant was referring to with those words. You refuse to make sense of the meaning of the word cadaver, said like that, with such coldness. Adriana and María exploded into cries. That type of news is staggering, it doesn't allow the horror of death to seep in.

EVERYONE KNEW THE OLD MAID who lived in apartment number eight as Aurorita. At 45 years old, she was still referred to with the diminutive because she was so kind. There was nothing she wouldn't do to help you.

When she lost interest in her soap operas and contemplated the "bad luck" of not having married, she spent her time leaning out the window and watching the people who walked up and down Calle Medellín. She invented names and professions; she imagined what everyone was like. No one knew why Aurorita had not found a husband. The neighbors blamed it on the mother she had been born to. Forever possessive, her mother thought that there was no man on earth good enough for her daughter. Others imagined that she had been so disillusioned by a love affair that she didn't want to have anything to do with love, and if she hadn't put on a habit it was thanks to the grief that the nuns in elementary school had caused her.

Even at her age, and in spite of being an old maid, doña Aurora, as the shopkeepers of the neighborhood called her, was a good looking woman. She always knew how to put her best foot forward against the unpleasantries of life.

But that fifth of November, when she went to the window after imagining what was going to happen in *The Rich Also Cry*, she saw an unexpected tragedy.

It was close to nine o'clock at night and only a few people were wandering around the streets. This made it possible for Aurora to recreate the story of exactly what she saw.

She watched a man walking; he was carrying a paper bag from the bakery. She tried to guess what bread he had bought. She remembered that her grandfather always used to say that people could be classified by their choice of pastries and bread.

The man stopped at the *quesadilla* stand, bought a few things and then began to walk down the street again. No one had noticed that a Volkswagen bus was following him closely. Even Aurorita was distracted, until the noises, the ruckus and the screams made her understand what she was witnessing.

As the man continued walking down the street, the VW kombi caught up with him, and when the back door opened, the heart-wrenching scream of a woman made the few people who were walking down Calle Medellín pay attention.

"Look out! Run!"

With those words, three armed men jumped swiftly out of the van and blocked the man's path. He let his bags of bread and *quesadillas* drop to the ground.

Aurorita opened her eyes as wide as she could. She knew that what she was witnessing was no trite episode of a soap opera. Shocked, she muffled a cry, and even though her mind ordered her to shut her eyes, much like she did when she was a little girl and something frightened her, she didn't miss one single detail of what happened two apartment buildings away.

Once they had blocked his way, the three men tried to force the man into the VW kombi. They wrestled unsuccessfully with him for a few seconds. From inside the vehicle a voice ordered the three attackers to do something, and they immediately shot at their opponent. The barrage of bullets shook the night, and before they took off at high speed, someone inside the VW kombi screamed.

It seemed like time had stopped—none of the witnesses said anything and no one approached the lifeless body on the asphalt.

Aurorita witnessed every last detail. Her eyes were glued to the corpse. For a moment, the impulse to escape into the void overtook her. Her mother, who from the other side of the apartment had heard the screams, shouted herself hoarse calling to her daughter, but Aurora didn't respond. Her ears weren't receiving any signals, the screams that preceded the tragedy kept resounding deep within her, shots that ended a life. From the street, no one noticed Aurora's petrified image. She had seen it all! She could identify the aggressors, the vehicle: the image had etched itself into her mind like a red-hot branding iron. The rest of the passers-by, including the woman who sold the *quesadillas*, preferred to get away from the area, to say they hadn't seen anything. Little by little curious onlookers began arriving from all around. Even though they hadn't witnessed the tragedy they wanted to participate in it, unlike those who had suffered through it.

Aurora's mother had to tug at her daughter's motionless body with great force. Stupefied, Aurora couldn't take her eyes off the dead man. It took a tremendous amount of effort to separate her from the window, to make her stop staring, to try to get her to come around, to provoke some reaction that would shake her out of her state of shock.

DAYS WENT BY before anyone knew anything about Aurorita. Her mother begged her—until she got sick and tired of it—to at least eat something, but Aurora couldn't even shake her head to say "no." She seemed numb. Her eyes remained as wide open as on that night. From time to time she moved around clumsily. The incident had completely transformed her. Sometimes a tear fell and gave her mother hope. She imagined that tears would breathe life back into her daughter.

For several months Aurora didn't utter a word. Her mother decided to secretly hide the reason behind her daughter's state of being. She didn't want anyone to know that her daughter had witnessed the assassination. She feared the authorities would bother her with ludicrous interrogations. She didn't want to go to the police station and it frightened her to think that those men, the assassins, could take vengeance on her daughter if she gave testimony as a witness. In any event, as much as she might have wanted to, Aurora couldn't denounce anyone. She couldn't do anything at all.

As time passed, Aurora recuperated, but she was never herself again—she was bitter. Observing death from a bedroom window and feeling powerless to do anything about it had left its impression on her forever. She blamed herself for many things—if she hadn't let her fantasies get hold of her, she could have warned that man. She felt like an accomplice to murder.

"WHAT NUMBER DID YOU USE to call him?"

Mama had told me beforehand to tell the truth. They knew all of Papa's moves, all of our moves, down to the "T." Ever since we stopped visiting Lecumberri, the phone had been tapped and from time to time a van would appear on the corner. The interrogation was just a formality, but perhaps it was also meant to be a lesson, to continue fomenting the horror.

"5-12-36-93."

"How often did you call him?"

There was a huge desk between us, with papers, guns, ashtrays, empty coffee cups. Mama was sitting next to me, cautious and attentive to the questions the chief of police was asking me.

"Once a week."

"What did you talk about?"

At that moment I felt like telling him to go to hell and running away. I wanted to go back to bed and get under the covers. Why such stupid questions, if all of our conversations had been recorded? Why fill out a report with my statements? I wanted to tell them to fuck off. I didn't know what to say, what to tell them about a conversation between a father and a son.

"About many things—the sale of subscriptions, school, the family . . . "

"How many times a month did you see him?"

Mama bit back her anger. As much as she had tried to prevent them from interrogating me, she couldn't stop it. Since I was the child that had had most contact with Papa, they imagined that I knew something that they ignored, as if he had talked to me about his aspirations, his projects.

"Sometimes once a month."

"What was your Papa's address?"

The office was constantly being invaded by court officials picking up reports, giving the boss messages, or simply passing through to get to the hallway that was at the other end of the office. From time to time, my interrogator turned to his notes to confirm what I had said. He kept his gaze on me, overflowing out of his armchair with his all-consuming attitude, perhaps imagining what his outer appearance caused me to feel inside, decoding the hatred, the affliction, the rage I held back.

"I never knew where he lived."

"Did you call him at another phone number?"

At first, they tried to get me to identify the body, to go into the room where it lay flat on the table. It was amongst the many already-decomposing bodies that were there on the floor. Mama gave an emphatic no. It was she, accompanied by David, who faced the stench of death.

The official ensconced in front of me appeared to be fulfilling his duty, his routine, the investigation. He more than knew the reasons, the motives that had ripped Papa's life away from him in the middle of the street. Life was no longer anything that I had been taught; it was now every human being's last opportunity.

WHEN YOU LOSE YOUR FATHER for the second time, at fifteen, you are accustomed to goodbyes. Your ability to absorb shock adjusts itself, so much so that the tragedy seems less painful.

Understand that now I look at everything through a lens. The transporting of the body to Puebla, the maddening moments at the wake, the public parade, the condolences, the guards, the gossip in the cafés, the heart-wrenching cries, the versions of stories recalling him as a good person, the recognition of his kindness, the whispers from person-to-person to find out how it happened. The looks that bore right through you, everything suggested resignation. Nevertheless, reality kept beating with every second. The difference is that confronting such events makes one more cautious, even colder. And in spite of everything, the machinations of repression continue to develop so that one comes to the understanding that death, as Papa would say, is the only certainty we have.

That Monday after the burial, at around ten o'clock in the morning, several of my classmates from high school arrived. At that age any old thing—and more so one of this magnitude—gives you a good reason to cut class.

Don Alberto, my best friend's father, accompanied my friends. Waiting for the right moment he took me off to a corner and, very solemnly, as he was accustomed to doing, he gave me some advice:

"Whoever did this, you shouldn't hate them."

His words seemed empty, meaningless, without rhyme or reason. It's impossible to behave in a Catholic manner and stop hating those who took away the ghost of your father. I didn't dare say anything, although I wanted to tell him to go to hell. What nerve giving me such shitty advice at a time like that, when the last thing you can think about is acquiescing, forgiving.

How do you overcome the powerlessness of such a fucked up piece of advice?

Will it ever be possible to forget those feelings I had found, the anger, the rage, the disgrace? Immersed in the moment, I couldn't say a thing. I didn't understand how he dared make that comment. With the passing of the years, however, I recognize the appropriateness of his words. When I recall what happened I am thankful for his apparent imprudence.

THE FUNERAL PROCESSION left the funeral home at 11:30 in the morning. Mama's decision, and that of all the children, was to accompany Papa on foot to the municipal cemetery. Curiously, I felt somewhat proud. It was the last time I would walk with him. I wished everyone could see us, I felt more like singing than crying. Now was the moment to know, that, in spite of everything, life isn't only full of tragedies.

Papa was walking by my side, singing, remembering.

FOR A LONG TIME I used to visit Papa's grave: I think it's good to know about your departed, to step on the ground that covers them, to smoke a cigarette in their company, even to tell them that in spite of everything you haven't stopped being amazed, that innocence still lives in your dreams. Taking your dead into consideration allows you to learn a bit more about yourself. You learn to live with what you inherit through blood, because you know that they decided, but you only received.

WE ALL WANTED TO FORGET the events, make it through the tragedy, let that sad story settle down.

"The dead, they are dead and that's that. You gain nothing by keeping their belongings." That had been the reasoning to my insistence.

Without too much persuasion, Mama accepted that Papa's belongings should not remain with those sons of bitches. It was my pressure, along with the support of Papa's half-sister that convinced her.

I so wanted to have that watch that Papa died with. It was an insignificant symbol, absurd even, but at that time there was nothing more important for me than to retrieve that object. Maybe it wasn't worth much; perhaps Papa had bought it for nothing at some open-air market. The value wasn't important at all—with that watch time had stood still for Papa. It didn't matter if it worked either, that object had accompanied him until his last second. I imagined the number of times that Papa would have fixed his gaze on its face. It was just one of those hopes that an adolescent could hold onto. I think it would have given me a great sense of security to put that watch on my wrist.

At last, after a lot of nagging, Mama agreed to go to the Attorney General's office, mostly to make me happy.

When we arrived in Mexico City, Papa's half-sister was already waiting for us at the bus station and we went together to the office. An undersecretary soon met us, and explained the series of procedures we would have to go through in order to obtain Papa's belongings.

The pile of paperwork began: the stamps, the signatures, the interviews, the notarized documents affirming that we were who we were. During those three hours, I continually touched my left wrist with the illusion that all of this trouble was worth the while. Perhaps I thought that by having that watch, Papa would always be with me.

When we thought that everything was in order, we returned to the first undersecretary. In spite of having flawlessly fulfilled all the prerequisites, he wanted to impose further requirements. Right then, propelled by her vulnerability, Papa's half-sister began to insult him, to scream at him at the top of her lungs, leaving him dumbfounded. He tried to say something but, in the midst of her transformation, Papa's half-sister didn't let him get a word in edgewise until after her explosion of hysteria. The supposed lawyer got up from his desk and began to walk down a long hallway that we could see from the counter.

Mama, who was still in shock as well, only had a short explanation from my aunt, which was meant to comfort her.

"This is how you have to treat these sons of bitches, sister."

After several minutes, the reprimanded clerk returned with Papa's file in his hands, along with a transparent plastic bag. He put the two items on top of the counter. The objects in the bag spilled out, the reports, the supposed investigations, the declarations were all strewn about. The clerk had acquiesced to our request but not without indicating his annoyance.

I searched for the watch with my eyes, but instead the photos of the dead body shot up in the middle of the street, the diagnoses, the autopsy report all jumped out.

Distressed at the spectacle, Mama suggested that I look the other way. Everything was there, a testimony to the end of Papa's days. The clothing, the photos, the reports, the inquiries, the details, the time, the events, the time, but not the watch. We had been naive to think that they had kept objects of any value, as little as that value might have been.

The undersecretary, when he discovered our surprise, felt satisfied. He had taken vengeance for the way in which my aunt had treated him minutes before. We were all silent. A wave of disappointment came over me—I had so wanted to have that watch. In the end I learned, without that object in my possession, that life is nothing but a sad illusion.

"GET DRUNK WITH THEM, shit, accept your ghosts, because if you try keeping them locked up in that chest, sooner or later they will bounce back at you. The fucking past, it's so screwy, learn to live with it."

You never really know how things happen, but I assure you that every member of my family has his or her own story. Each one recreates his or her own version, his or her own way of getting close to the events, of digesting them. Each one takes hold of the city, of the story, of life, as best as he or she can, or, perhaps, in the most convenient way.

In spite of the fact that memories never come back on their own, there are times when I let myself listen to their voices. There is always something that brings them out, that jolts them back into your mind: a song, a phrase, a street, a name, a person, any old detail manages to bring the past into the present, to recreate what we were.

You allow this coexistence with ghosts when you open the door for them and tell them to go to hell, when you scream and cry. In the long run you'll have to accept whatever comes and stop blaming the past. It's better to celebrate it, and on occasion, even in the most painful way, enjoy it.

I often go to the places where memories exist. I like the San Francisco neighborhood, where they sell stuffed *tortillas*.

Before Papa gave up everything for his ideals, we would go as a family every Sunday to eat in San Francisco: consommé, rice with a fried egg, and *chalupas*. To conclude the routine, Papa called the meringue seller and he flipped a coin for a few desserts. Sometimes we got more desserts, other times the tray of pastries passed by without reaching our palate. The relaxing Sundays of a middle-class family, the kids in private schools, matinees and our own business. The problems didn't change daily life, there would always be debts to pay and as a compensation some commodities: walks, pats on the back. Life back then was always in front of us, we simply had to reach out for it.

THE DAY BEFORE Papa changed his life I accompanied him to San Francisco to have the car washed. That Sunday the family couldn't keep its weekly date. Mama was home in bed, sick with hepatitis. Papa and I took the walk alone.

While the others did their job, Papa and I savored some strawberries with cream in the same restaurant as always. That would be our goodbye. The next morning he left the house in search of his utopia. I suppose he knew then that a few hours later, his life, my life, the life of our entire family would change.

As the years have gone by, I have come to realize that it was such a touching way of saying good-bye without saying it; we talked about so many things. At the age of ten, your idea of fatherhood is full of heroism, you question nothing, you boast about your dad in school and you feel protected. I suppose that there were few times that we got along like that.

The way each one of us gets close to our parents is so different, the concepts we create so diverse. In your case with Papa, Irving, someone stole that opportunity from you.

I have often thought about the circumstances, the facts, why things happen as they do and not any other way. It's obvious that our future is not pre-determined, but how do coincidences weave together? Perhaps the facts are always the same and history, more than a series of events, is a digestive, circular result. It could be that the ones who change are the protagonists themselves.

A week before Papa was assassinated, he came to Puebla for a visit. María, Adriana and I had a great time that Sunday, in his company. We walked around the city like we had seldom done, and as usual, we went to San Francisco to eat. We even went to visit the mummy of San Sebastián de Aparicio. It's not that we were Catholic anymore; it was more like we wanted to rummage through all the nooks and crannies as an excuse to be together.

As always there were coin tosses at the end of the meal. We all recalled the good old times. It would be five years before we repeated that Sunday tradition.

The coincidence that Papa chose the same place to say goodbye, on a Sunday, with the same surroundings, seemed to confirm that goodbyes apparently have a specific time and place.

As long as you are alive the constant face of death is present on every street corner. You can always look for explanations for the coincidences: Papa said goodbye to me on two occasions. The difference was that the second time I had lost the ability to be shocked.

Talking with you now about these things, explaining everything that you didn't know then, everything that belonged to you, just like to every one else in the family, curiously enough doesn't make the memories bang around in my head like on other occasions. They don't crash into each other. It would seem that I am warming up to them, hoping that they will let me, that they will console me from the truth. Because from time to time it's a good thing to breathe life back into the dead folks in our memories, into objects, situations, events.

When you come to the end of your memory and your pupils try to acclimate to the luminosity, you remain face to face with the person who supposedly invited your Papa to participate in the guerrilla. You feel like you have the right to recriminate him, to blame him for what happened, just as if Papa had been a child who was forced to do what he did. So you pardon him, even, from the responsibility of abandoning you. I've always asked myself who suffered the least—if it was me, who lost Papa on more than one occasion, or you, who only had him for a brief moment. The story didn't take you alone by surprise. We all suffered from it in our own way, and if you don't give yourself the chance to live that suffering you're fucked. Neither you nor anyone else was a stranger to the events.

You've said that you learned to play with your loneliness, that very few times you felt a part of the family because you didn't suffer the same, or better yet, you suffered in a different way. I think it was time that played with each of us under a different set of rules.

I can't imagine how many times the word "Papa" didn't make sense in your reality. There are no words to console you. Each of us suffered in our own way, each of us lives with the ghosts as best we can, and we play the cards and recreate the story, putting into place, in a terrible way, each piece of the puzzle.

Perhaps that is what life is.

About the Author

Fritz Glockner

Puebla, Mexico, 1961. Professor of creative writing at the *Benemérita Universidad Autónoma de Puebla*. In the United States, he has been a guest at the Clark University Latin American Film Festival, and has taught at the University of Iowa, and at Dartmouth College. A journalist and researcher who specializes in the so called "Mexican War of Low-Intensity" of the 1960's, '70's and '80's. He has published: *Un pueblo en campaña*, 1995; *Cementerio de Papel*, 2004 (made into a movie in 2009); *Memoria Roja (historia de la guerrilla en México 1943-1968)*, 2007 & 2013; *El barco de la Ilusión*, 2005 (made into a movie in 2009); *Se nos hizo tarde*, 2008.

This novel *Returning from the Underground* [*Veinte de Cobre (memoria de la clandestinidad)*, original title] published in 1996, 1997, 2004, 2010, was his first incursion into the Mexican dirty war theme, and provides the framework for Guillermo Arriaga's movie *Amores Perros*. In the words of the famous Mexican novelist, journalist, and playwright, Vicente Leñero, this is: "A little great novel, indispensable for the understanding of the dirty war of the 1970s."

About the Translator

Photo: Eli S. Burakian

Elizabeth Polli
Taught Spanish language and literature, and was the Spanish Language Program Director at Dartmouth College from 1998 until 2014.

She began translating for the film industry in the 1980s, while in Spain. Her publications include translations of poetry, prose and essays by Sergio Chejfec, Felix de la Concha, Fritz Glockner, Ana Merino, José María Merino, Luis Muñoz, Wendy Guerra and Keiselim A. Montás. Her translations of scholarly essays on comics have appeared in the "International Journal of Comic Art." Elizabeth is also an avid knitter.

Zompopos
El libro es un Zompopo

Returning From The Underground
by Fritz Glockner, translated from the
Spanish by Elizabeth Polli, was completed
in January 2018, in New Hampshire.

The Zompopos Project
Élitro Editorial del Proyecto Zompopos
(El libro es un Zompopo)
New York – New Hampshire

Other books by **The Zompopos Project**:

Amor de ciudad grande (2006)	**Keiselim A. Montás**
Allá (diario del transtierro) (2012)	**Keiselim A. Montás**
Cuando el resto se apaga (2013)	**Kianny N. Antigua**
Islamabad queda al norte (2014)	**Jimmy Valdez-Osaku**
En sus pupilas una luna a punto de madurar (2015)	**José Gustavo Melara**
Como el agua (colección de Haikus) (2016)	**Keiselim A. Montás**
Like Water (A Haiku Collection) (2017)	**Keiselim A. Montás**
Hacia Yukahú (poemas, 2017)	**Ricardo Cabrera**
ANAGAMI (poemas, 2017)	**José Kozer**

All available at: http://editorialzompopos.blogspot.com/

El Proyecto Zompopos: Este proyecto promulga al Zompopo (hormiga corta hojas / atta cephalotes) como un símbolo de cooperación entre los humanos y nuestro medio ambiente, identificando intereses comunes en necesidades, cultura, lenguaje e ideales. Propone un auto-examen de nuestra cotidianidad y una revisión de nuestras formas de consumo para dar nuevos usos a objetos que normalmente desechamos.

The Zompopos Project: This Project champions the Zompopo (leaf cutting ant / atta cephalotes) as a symbol of cooperation amongst humans and our living environment by finding common ground via needs, culture, language and ideals. It proposes a look at our daily lives and a revision of our modes of consumption in order to find uses for objects we would normally discard.